RINE POOK ESQUIRE

MARINE POOK ESQUIRE

What a shock for Pook! What a blow for Honners! It's happened at last. As the massive Japanese war-machine remorselessly advances westward the Royal Marines are rushed to a remote desert island in the Indian Ocean to construct a defence base against the enemy.

Pook and Honners are the weak links in this scheme, and characteristically Honners' first action is to establish a lucrative trading-post, while Pook organises a dance for some visiting nurses and predictably falls in love with the gorgeous Pamela.

Running through the story is the shadow of that brilliant tactician Lieutenant Tudor and his shaky Section as they struggle through Exercise Chop-sticks and Exercise Mad Dogs in a vain attempt to increase their combat efficiency.

The extraordinary adventures that befall Pook and Honners under Sergeant Canyon on this tropical island provide a steady tide of laughter, with the additional bonus of a surprise ending.

Compulsive reading for servicemen and laymen alike, as Pook reveals the other side of war with his original wit and humour.

Peter Pook titles available from Emissary
(in the order in which they were originally published)

Banking on Form
Pook in Boots
Pook in Business
Pook Sahib
Bwana Pook
Professor Pook
Banker Pook Confesses
Pook at College
Pook's Tender Years
Pook and Partners
Playboy Pook
Pook's Class War
Pook's Tale of Woo
Pook's Eastern Promise
Beau Pook Proposes
Pook's Tours
The Teacher's Hand-Pook
Gigolo Pook
Pook's Love Nest
Pook's China Doll
Pook's Curiosity Shop
Marine Pook Esquire
Pook's Viking Virgins

MARINE POOK ESQUIRE

PETER POOK

EMISSARY PUBLISHING
P.O. Box 33, Bicester, OX26 4ZZ, UK.

First published in Great Britain 1978
by Robert Hale Ltd., London.

First published in paperback in 1999 by
Emissary Publishing, P.O. Box 33, Bicester, OX26 4ZZ, UK.
This edition published 2006

British Library Cataloguing-in-Publication Data.
A catalogue record for this book is available from the British Library.

ISBN: 1-874490-71-6
ISBN-13: 978-1-874490-71-5

©Peter Pook 1978
Front Cover Illustration: Richie Perrott

Produced by: Manuscript ReSearch (Book Producers),
P.O. Box 33, Bicester, OX26 4ZZ, U.K.
Tel: 01869 323447/322552
Printed and bound by MWL Print Group Ltd., South Wales.

To our magnificent Royal Marines
—despite Pook and Honners

ONE

"As your Chief Intelligence Officer I do solemnly declare that this hell ship's position is exactly *here*," Honners announced confidently, stabbing the Admiralty chart with an Italian bayonet to pinpoint us two hundred miles east of Durban.

A delighted gasp of admiration arose from the Marines clustered round him on the mess-deck of the troopship *Moon of Mandalay*. Previous visits had taught us that Durban—and South Africa generally—was the answer to the sailor's prayer for wine, women and song, being Nature's reply to war.

"How on earth did you manage to work it out, Honners?" I asked, for we were under the strict security clamp of the top brass and had not sighted land since we had been spewed out of the Red Sea and the Gulf of Aden some two weeks earlier.

"Just luck, my simple friends, coupled with a deep knowledge of navigation, the stars, the tides and two sensitive ears when sweeping the bridge," Honners smirked superiorly. "As I forecast back in Egypt this is a Blighty ship, taking us home after the rigours of war such as few men have experienced before. A glorious week in Durban to restore our shattered nerves and battle-weary bodies—then pipe all hands for a UK draft!"

Gabby Ellington was slitting his sharp eyes at the horizon across the mirror-calm waters. "Then how come the land is flat? What I remember most about South Africa was the mountains."

"Not all Africa is mountainous, little idiot boy. Large chunks of it are as flat as your head. Your master has spoken and I am not in the habit of making erroneous calculations. You may pay homage to me in the bar later."

"Look out—Crusher!" I warned..

Like a conjuring trick Honners concertina'd the chart and stuffed it up the leg of his shorts. Sergeant Crusher Canyon had already put him on punishment fatigues for the rest of the war but stealing an Admiralty chart from the bridge was a cells' job.

Crusher's great bulk lumbered up to observe us quietly playing cards on the mess-table. "I brings you good tidings, men," he rumbled.

"You've been posted back to Egypt?" Honners inquired.

"Even better, Marine the Hon. Lesley Pilkington-Goldberg, CB and Order of the Mouth. See that land through the porthole on the starboard beam, men?"

"Let me guess, Sergeant. The Isle of Wight?"

"Not quite, Honners. It's a place that will go down in history as the Marines' Graveyard."

"Don't tell me it's Deal Barracks!"

Sergeant Canyon chuckled. "The Loyota Islands."

"Hooray! Big deal! Everybody cheer. Never heard of them. Are they off the coast of South Africa?"

"South Africa! You gone sick or something? We're thousands of miles from South Africa—in fact we're thousands of miles from any place. If you was an albatross you might eventually sight Java. This dump is so remote that you won't get no mail for at least three months because even the Fleet Post Office don't know where it is. They don't even know it exists yet."

"Are they hiding us away? Have we been sent to Coventry? Is the Admiralty cross with us because of the nasty things we said in our letters home about the grub?"

"Don't talk wet, Honners. They've chosen us because they know nobody can kill us, see. They know we're a unique Section because we fought in Greece and Crete against the Germans, then in North Africa against the Italians and never so much as got wounded."

"Only because we used our loaf all the time, Sergeant."

"Three of the bloodiest campaigns in the history of war, yet Number 3 Section come out without a scratch, not a man lost, not a man hurt."

"I sustained a severe wound in Crete," Honners reminded him.

"Yes, cut your mouth on a beer can. They predicted sixty per cent casualties, yet all our lot got took off to a man. One extra if we count that girl Pook had in tow."

"War has taken its toll on me though. Covered from head to toe in dhobi rash."

"Nobody's suffered more than me," I protested. "I'm one mass of prickly heat."

Gabby grimaced. "How would you like my foot-rot?"

"What about me then?" Corporal Puffy Crood moaned. "Galloping dysentery is murder. How would you like to go to the toilet twenty-eight times a day?"

Tilty Slant sighed nostalgically. "You should worry. I haven't been for twenty-eight days."

"I wish to report a peculiar malfunction of my sexual organs," Dennis Long exclaimed. "I haven't liked to mention it before but I can't get married if there's no cure. It's a kind of Derbyshire Droop, as though I'm impotent. I daren't tell my fiancée back home."

Marine Ackland, our bugler, spoke up worriedly. "I may have to give up music, Sergeant. Ever since the bombing we took in Crete I've suffered from a nervous stomach. I can't stop it, but every time I blow my bugle I fart in time with the notes. Last time I blew reveille Lieutenant Titterton put me on a charge for disorderly conduct. I won't describe what lengths I've gone to trying to stop it but it gets worse."

Sergeant Canyon rubbed his blue jaw as he listened to the familiar catalogue of tropical ailments. "Well, men, soon your aches and pains will be over because we're being dumped on an uninhabited desert island like you sees on the movies. And if anyone leaves it alive he'll be shot for cowardice in the face of the enemy."

"What enemy?" Honners snapped, voicing all our thoughts.

"The Japanese," Crusher leered triumphantly.

"The Japs!" we gasped incredulously. "They'll kill us!"

"The Japs are advancing on all fronts, men. It is your duty and privilege to stop them. Admittedly it is a dangerous mission. Statistically you are outnumbered. For example, Honners alone will find himself pitted against twenty-three thousand soldiers, so it will indeed be a fight to the death."

"Not with those odds—they won't even be able to find me to fight it out."

"Now, men, prepare to disembark. Honners, you take the basket of carrier-pigeons, the crossbow and the dagger."

Honners looked aghast. "Carrier-pigeons, crossbow and dagger! What is this—the Crusades? Why don't you give me a pike too?"

"You don't understand this new type of warfare, Honners. We have to kill silently by night, see. The pigeons can't be detected like radio, so we can transmit messages without the Japs listening in to our chat."

"But the last time I opened the basket they flew off and we never saw them again. What good is that?"

"Pigeons don't come back—they only fly home. It's

strictly one way communication, see. Also, if you're desperate for food you can eat them, see."

"Not much point in getting hungry after message time then. I'll keep mine for supper and deliver the messages by hand."

"Now the steel crossbow enables you to kill at a distance in complete silence—vital when you're outnumbered—and the dagger lets you kill at close quarters, again in silence, see."

"Why don't you give me a horse shod with rubber shoes? Then I could creep on to the battlefield and take the enemy tanks by surprise, pull out my modern mace and smash them to pieces. Then I could mow down the infantry with my sling. No wonder we're losing this war left right and centre."

Sergeant Canyon turned to me. "Marine Pook Esquire— as you likes to be known as to distinguish you from the regulars—you are our trained diver, so your first task will be to blow a gap in the coral reef wide enough for the invasion barges to go in and land."

I laughed modestly. "But I'm only a fun diver, Sergeant. Bournemouth beach and swimming-pool stuff."

"Listen, Pook. You don't have to dive to the bottom of the Pacific Ocean, see. You merely plants the explosives on the reef, not two thousand feet down in the unknown. Most of the time you won't even be out of your depth. You only needs the mask in case you get dizzy with fear and falls in."

"But I could get blown up and killed, Sergeant."

"The only way you can get killed is by refusing to do it. We don't explode the charge while you're sitting on it— you comes up first, then we use a detonator."

"I still say it's highly dangerous. Why don't we wait for high tide and sail over the reef?"

"Because it's only at high tide that we can get in at all, Pook, even with the reef blown."

"So wait for low tide and tackle the reef with pick and shovel."

"Or we could dig a tunnel under the reef, eh?" Crusher sneered. "Just you obey orders and blast the reef. My oath, no wonder we never lost a man in action! They're saying service in our Section is safer than joining the Land Army on a Welsh farm."

"Sergeant," Honners called from the porthole, "I can see several islands now. Perhaps we can find one without a reef round it. Why do it the hard way?"

"This is Loyota Atoll for your information, Vasco da Gama. There are seven islands in it—and every one has a coral reef. Why? Because that's how coral islands are formed. Why? Ask all them little bugs what build them up."

"You probably mean the calcareous skeletons of Anthozoa and Hydrozoa," Honners sniffed. "They accumulate to construct three types of reefs: fringing, barrier and atolls."

Sergeant Canyon hurred. "I don't care what they call the cow, so long as Pook blows it clear for our craft to land. Remember that we are the first white men to settle on the island and the highest point above sea-level is only eight feet."

"And it is liberally covered with cocos nucifera and musa sapientum."

"What in hell's that, you little show-off?"

"Everybody knows they are coconut-palms and banana plants, surely. Of course, I was assuming we all speak the same language."

"Two can play that game, Honners—we are now part of MNBDO, got it?"

"Marines' New British Dhobi Organization? They've made us the Fleet Laundry!"

"Mobile Naval Base Defence Organization, stupid. So we build a base for the fleet until we're overwhelmed. Not a man leaves here alive, see."

"Too bad, because I am putting in a chittee for permission to return to Cairo for a hearing-aid."

"You what!"

"I beg your pardon? See, my hearing is defective since all that bombing and gunfire in Crete. That's why I can never obey orders. I can't catch what you and Titterton keep shouting at me."

"Then hear this down your little ear-trumpet—the only way you'll leave here is in an extremely short coffin covered with a Union Jack."

"So don't blame me if I don't hear the Retreat when we attack the Japs."

"We'll be damned lucky if you hear the order to advance, mate, never mind the Retreat. Now, men, on a mission such as this what do we need above all things?"

"Immediate repatriation, Sergeant," I suggested. "We haven't been home for a whole year."

"We need what the Royal Marines have always been famous for. You all know what it is from your study of the Corps' history dating back to 1664."

"Compassionate leave, Sergeant?" Dennis ventured. Dennis's fiancee, Veronica, had written to him every day since we left England and we knew from the numbers on the back of the envelopes that she had reached the 360 mark. Following our withdrawal from Crete in 1941 Dennis received a bundle of 57 letters from her, delayed by the German invasion of the island.

"I'll give you a clue, men," Crusher rumbled. "First, what is the Corps' motto?"

"Splice the main brace, Sergeant," I barked smartly.

"Good grief, Pook, surely you knows by now it's Per Mare Per Terram—By Sea and By Land. It's wrote on your badge, lad."

"Sorry, Sergeant. I thought that was the name of the firm who made them."

"Now what did George Forster say to Captain James Cook about the Jollies in 1774 anybody?"

"Disband them, Jim?" I suggested.

Sergeant Canyon sighed. "Sometimes I wonder if I've been posted to the Royal Corps of Idiots, Pook. George Forster remarked on our extraordinary bond of comradeship. He called it our esprit de corps."

"That was a long time ago, Sergeant. When did we lose it?"

Crusher snorted. "Lost it! Why, it's stronger than ever today. That's why the Bootnecks are the finest regiment in the world."

"My family wanted me to be a Kamikaze pilot," Honners observed. "So they had to settle for the Marines."

"And they done right too because the Nazis call us Churchill's Butchers."

"I used to be a butcher in real life," Tilty Slant told us.

"This is real life, Slant. You'll get no quarter from the Japs any more than the Jerries, believe me. So, men, what must our watchword be on the Loyota Islands?"

"Run for our lives," Honners said confidently.

"Ah, but you can't run far on a tiny island. That's why we must intensify our training programme, see."

"Swimming lessons every day."

"Learn to speak Japanese," I added.

"Make our own Japanese uniforms," Gabby insisted.

"Boat-building," Dennis suggested.

"Rowing practice," Tilty advised.

We all stood to attention as Lieutenant Titterton entered the mess with that severe frown of one who is determined to be a born leader of men despite rosy cheeks and slightly knock-knees. We assumed expressions of hardened battle campaigners ready to follow him to the death, but at heart we all knew we were really civilians dressed up in uniform whose sole aim was to avoid death and go home to our families. So far we had been pretty successful in Europe and North Africa, attacking enemy positions with ferocity, only to find they had gone, then falling back to flush them out until we discovered we were accidentally clear of the battle areas and surrounded by civilians. One memorable action ended in all our Section being driven back by the enemy to a function held by the WVS, where we danced and drank the night away. During another battle we lost contact with the opposing forces to the extent that we were compelled to rest in a nightclub, of which several of us became members. On another occasion we advanced so far along the desert that when Lieutenant Titterton gave the order to charge we found ourselves in the suburbs of Cairo, so we explored the Great Pyramid of Cheops, had camel rides and saw *Gone With The Wind* at the cinema.

Lieutenant Titterton, late of Pegasus Insurance Co. Ltd., had behind him a unique service record in that during Officer Training Exercises he had been routed by his deadly rival, Lieutenant Tudor, to the tune of three retreats—one of which required us to seek sanctuary in Salisbury Cathedral—and two complete annihilations of his troops. Lieutenant

Titterton himself had been killed seven times; eight if one counted suicide rather than capture. Under his command Number 3 Section had become known as The Prisoners for obvious reasons, except on the notable occasion when we had escaped capture by sheltering in a mine-field.

To improve his military efficiency Lieutenant Titterton played chess against himself every night and read *Remplir on Strategy* by day, even on the toilet. His hero was the Duke of Wellington, whom he tried to look like without a horse, and he struggled to emulate the Iron Duke's ability to inspire his men and dominate a whole army. We tried to help him by staring at him as though we were hypnotized by his martial bearing and often remarking in his hearing how he inspired us. This was far from easy for Lieutenant Titterton was short, shy, chubby and blushed readily, and we knew everything about him from his batman, Tilty Slant. For instance, we knew that he liked fancy underwear and that his girlfriend called him Chubsy. Finally, it had not escaped our notice that in action Lieutenant Titterton lost much of the Duke of Wellington's aura, running about like a blue-arse fly to find out what was happening, screaming highly unprofessional orders like "Where the devil's all that banging coming from?" and in the last analysis glad to follow his men rather than lead them, provided they knew the way out.

However, his personal courage was never in question, for he would have been killed long ago if men like Honners, Gabby, Tilty, Dennis and I had not possessed the presence of mind to practically carry him bodily away from the enemy when his miscalculations led us to their vicinity.

Lieutenant Titterton stood uncomfortably at attention, like Napoleon trying to forget Waterloo, waiting for his glance to mesmerize us. I did my best to look mesmerized and inspired simultaneously, waiting to hear what Remplir had to say about Islands, defence of. His theme seemed to be that we must be prepared to die in order to improve our statistical record back at HQ, who had severely reprimanded us for upsetting their casualty predictions with our Killed in Action, Nil; Wounded, Nil; Taken Prisoner, Nil. Ours was the sole Section with a clean sheet, whereas war was a dangerous business in which casualties were expected even demanded. Conversely, we were the unhealthiest Section in the Regiment, with a sickness rate far above the average. We were bedevilled by every ailment known to man except pregnancy, and Honners had been singled out as the un-healthiest man in the war, being more in the nature of an invalid than a combatant. It was a suspicious factor, Lieutenant Titterton emphasized, that Honners paraded as fit for active service only immediately prior to leave periods, then returned from those furloughs with fresh diseases as though his hobby was collecting them. How was it, he demanded, that Honners was the only man in the Regiment to have been actually banned from the surgeries and hospitals of Egypt on the grounds that he considered himself a full-time patient?

"You should be aware that, owing to excessive gunfire in Crete, I am presently applying for a hearing-aid," Honners interrupted.

"Silence, man!"

"And as such an appliance can only be fitted in Cairo, or better still UK, I request to be drafted home imme-diately...."

"I ordered you to be silent, Honners."

"Your lips are moving but I hear nothing," Honners

wailed, cupping hand to ear and leaning forward. "How can I obey orders when those guns have sent me deaf?"

"Even on this troopship you have persistently reported sick with dhobi rash and athlete's foot, not to mention bothering the MO with dandruff. Imagine it! I command a top combat unit and one of my men can't fight because he has dandruff!"

"Remember my prickly heat, sir," I reminded him.

"And my foot-rot," Gabby cried.

"I've got Derbyshire Droop," Dennis moaned.

"I practically live in the toilets," Puffy groaned.

"I haven't been for weeks," Tilty winced.

"My nervous fart makes me scared to blow the bugle," Marine Ackland wailed.

"Shut up!" Lieutenant Titterton screamed, clenching his fists. "Whenever I address you, whatever I say, you seem to think I am your local GP. You are obsessed with your minor ailments like hypochondriacs of the worst sort. I often feel I am commanding an intensive-care unit—men who are so ill that sometimes they are unable to reach the sick-bay unaided. Last time Honners caught a cold he requested me to lay on an ambulance and stretcher so he could witness some football match or other. Now, any questions before we get on with the real business of the day?"

"When will the new sick-bay be operational on the island?" Honners inquired. "You see, the confined space on this floating slum has given me splitting claustrophobic headaches. . . ."

Honners was silenced by Crusher's huge hand being clamped round his mouth and face, coupled with vice grip round the back of his neck, always dubbed by Honners as Crusher's passion for our right of free speech.

Lieutenant Titterton went into briefing pose, legs apart and holding his cane with both hands so he could bend it like a coathanger.

As usual his talk fell flat because he merely repeated everything Sergeant Canyon had told us just before, although, as usual, he was unaware of this. But unfortunately this occurred time and again because if Sergeant Canyon didn't beat him to it Tilty Slant did. As batman, Tilty often knew more than anybody, including Lieutenant Titterton, and what Tilty didn't know Honners did because our Unit was a nest of espionage. Tilty read all Lieutenant Titterton's mail, official and private, in and out, while he was working in the officer's cabin, then conferred with his fellow batmen in case he had missed any buzzes. This information was passed to us and added to by Honners.

Honners' method was to carry a broom, so that wherever officers were talking he would sweep round them, leaving little piles of dirt everywhere. His broom enabled him to penetrate otherwise forbidden areas, such as the wardroom and the bridge. In his pocket was a duster for polishing zones of information like the Captain's table and Colonel Tank's office. Paradoxically, one of the charges which had put Honners on permanent punishment fatigues was loitering in unlawful places and reading classified documents. The others included malingering, absent without leave, sleeping on duty and pleading deafness when given orders. He also claimed that a physical deformity restricted the use of his right arm to the extent that he was unable to salute officers, and a saline allergy prevented his going to sea. In the North African desert he suffered a kind of hay fever caused by sand, and Greece was so dry that he developed asthma. I think his worst folly occurred when he was sentenced to pack-drill for leaving the column and going off in a wide arc, claiming that he could not march straight because one of his legs was shorter than the other as a result of what he called rifle rickets.

Lieutenant Titterton struggled on with his stale news, baffled why we were not astounded and excited by his revelation of our new orders. Why, he repeatedly asked himself, could he not hypnotize and inspire his troops instead of boring them to the point where he could barely hold their attention. Even in the field they tended to ignore him, so that he was required to bawl, wave his arms, and jump up and down to attract their notice.

"Any questions, men?" he inquired on the completion of his homily about dying for England and making it a safe land for our loved ones to live in.

"I wish to ask a question in the form of a statement," Honners piped up in his high piercing voice. "Let it be quite clearly understood that my illustrious uncle, Admiral Sir Graham Pilkington-Goldberg, VC, DSO, RAC, AA and Co-op, Seventh Sea Lord of the Admiralty at the last count of heads, will be severely displeased when he hears from me that his favourite nephew is not only going deaf but has been denied his right to be fitted with an Aid, hearing, Royal Marine, for the use of. Furthermore. . . ."

Lieutenant Titterton literally snarled at Honners upon hearing Admiral Sir Graham Pilkington-Goldberg thrown at him once more, shouting back at him so loudly that he ended in a fit of coughing, "Damn your hearing-aid, Honners, but I can assure you that such a surprise is waiting for you on Loyota Atoll that the last thing you will require will be any instrument for sharpening your senses!"

TWO

After I had assisted in blowing a gap in the coral reef our invasion barges with their flat bottoms were able to beach quite comfortably. While we disembarked our gear all the bilge water was pumped from the *Moon of Mandalay* through an eight-inch pipe into a huge static water tank on the beach. At first we thought this was to be a miniature swimming pool until Sergeant Canyon explained that as the island possessed no water this was for drinking and cooking. All we had to do was to chlorinate it, then boil it.

"Then throw it away," I suggested.

"You won't throw much away when you're thirsty, Pook. Life is tough on a tiny desert island, believe me, mate. There's sweet Fanny Adams here and the only thing there's plenty of is damn-all. You eats from the tin and sleeps rough, see. No money and nothing to buy with it, see. Back to Early Man in his cave, you might say. Your palmy days up the desert and around the Suez Canal are over, Pook. When they says back to square one this is it, see. In a word we're stuck on a lump of coral surrounded by sharks."

We had seen the sharks on the way in, anything up to eighteen feet in length, as well as several giant turtles lazing in the ocean. Flying-fish splattered the surface, often landing on the decks, while far out to sea a whale spouted hugely. In the clear depths swam multitudes of fish, particularly angel-fish and eels. The whole area seemed alive with marine activity.

"I observe the cocos nucifera to be swarming with pteropus edulis," Honners remarked airily.

"Do you always talk like that, Honners, or did your dad cosh you with a dictionary as a child to shut you up?"

Sergeant Canyon inquired. "You don't so much cackle as throw up."

"I was merely drawing your attention to the fact that the coconut-palms are full of flying foxes—the monster bats with the five-foot wing-span which live on fruit. You should have one on your shoulder in lieu of a parrot."

"If I had you on my shoulder it would be better than any parrot, Honners. You even looks like one."

"I've never seen a parrot perched on a gorilla before."

"You give me much more lip like that and your nose will walk into my fist and bust itself all over your pan."

Lieutenant Titterton came bustling up to announce that our tents had been unloaded, so we could erect them two men to one tent. Each tent measured seven feet square, sufficent to contain two camp-beds and allow for a small space between each. Honners chose our site in a small gully which he said would shelter us from the wind. Then he went to work with a will, cursing and screaming at the structure as though it was a living creature. Time after time the canvas enveloped him like a parcel, when he appeared to be actually fighting it.

"It's supposed to be a tent, Honners," I advised him when he had resorted to kicking it after falling about the clearing draped in canvas as though it was some monster wedding dress, "not a mobile obstacle course."

"For my money the damned thing is a collapsible bungalow," Honners swore.

All around us neat square tents were going up, beds being erected, mosquito-nets being hung, yet we were still at ground-level. "Ours is obviously defective, Peter," Honners decided.

"I reckon it is now."

"Our best bet is to leave it flat and sleep under it like an eiderdown—it's got at least twelve walls and three tops. Between you and me I think we've been issued with a parachute by mistake."

"All the other tents are square, Honners. I think where you've gone wrong is trying to erect it in the shape of a wigwam."

"*I've* gone wrong! You cheeky guttersnipe! When we unpacked it you thought the bag was the tent. Then I got one end up and you cried 'Oh look—there's a skylight in the roof!' That's the flap for the door, idiot."

Eventually Corporal Crood and Marine Ackland came along to assist us. These two friends seemed capable of doing anything and getting it right first time. After ten minutes they had the tent erected with guy-ropes stretched, but then Honners had to visit the makeshift sick-bay to be treated for mild concussion and shock because he tripped over five guy-ropes in quick succession to perform a kind of acrobatic routine, shrieking, "Imagine building council houses, then surrounding them with trip-wires!"

As a result of the delay Honners obtained the last of the camp-beds, the defective one. It had been broken in transit and had assumed the peculiar curvature of an airplane propeller, so that while Honners' head and chest tended to fall off one side when he lay on it, his hips and legs fell off the other side.

"It's like trying to sleep on a science-fiction mouse-trap," he shouted angrily every time he woke up lying across the bed through falling off both sides simultaneously. "I'll try sleeping on the floor before this thing breaks my back in two."

"How about your mosquito-net, Honners? Could be

dangerous without it," I warned.

"Forget it. I'm too bushed to go out catching mosquitoes tonight, matey."

Our first night on the island was unforgettable. Despite the sleep of exhaustion we were awakened by Honners' unique oath ringing round the camp. "Berrrrrr . . . luddy . . . hell!"

I jumped out of bed with shock, to find Honners bashing the camp-bed with the butt-end of his rifle. "Light! Give me a light, somebody!"

"I can't find the matches," I cried.

"This is no time to have a smoke. Flash the torch."

"What's wrong, Honners?"

"What's wrong! Only a giant python on my bed!"

"Come off it. Probably the local grass-snake."

"It might have been the local maggot, but it was ten feet long. Slithered right over me."

"I expect we're pitched on their run, like rabbits have."

"So we can expect them to be passing back and forth all night then? Perhaps this is Snake junction."

Lieutenant Titterton burst into the tent to ascertain the cause of the disturbance. "Well, Honners—I might have known it would have to be you—what do you mean by arousing the entire camp with your noise?"

"Despite my iron nerves I am not in the habit of remaining silent when my tent becomes a snake-pit," Honners retorted. "One does not normally turn over again and drop off to sleep after a giant python has slithered over one."

"Rubbish, man. Probably a tree snake."

"If the trees around here harbour fifteen-foot snakes somebody else can climb up and cut the coconuts."

"Honners, you must realize you are no longer residing in the security and comfort of your ancestral home. On this island we shall meet with snakes, scorpions, lizards and other unfamiliar creatures, so you must learn to live with them."

"Then you have them in your tent to live with you. I might have been swallowed and all you would have done is to post me as missing, believed eaten."

"Don't exaggerate, you stupid little fellow. Why isn't your mosquito-net erected as per orders?"

"Because I can't erect my bed as per orders. It's defective and I get thrown out both sides because it curls up at the ends and warps."

"Do you know what happens to men who are bitten by mosquitoes?"

"They get malaria and have to be sent back to civilization."

"I've been bitten fifty-six times, sir," I informed Lieutenant Titterton.

"Good heavens, Pook! Is your net defective?"

"No, sir. The mozzies went for me this afternoon. They seem to like me."

"So at last you have found something which likes you, eh?"

"There's almost fifty-six mosquitoes inside my net, sir," Dennis observed worriedly.

"Can't you get us some anti-mosquito cream, sir?" Tilty wondered.

"When will the new sick-bay be open to do something about my dhobi-rash?" Honners moaned.

"Do you think charcoal biscuits would absorb some of the wind in my stomach, sir?" Marine Ackland inquired.

Lieutenant Titterton tried to contain his chagrin without screaming. "Silence, men! No matter what happens day or night all you seem to worry about are your petty ailments. For pity sake try to forget them and remember we are here to fight the Japanese to the death."

"How can we die if we're sick, sir?" I asked.

"But you're for ever sick—the lot of you. You've been sick since the day you were called up. Yet we've not lost a man in action, not had a man wounded."

"Nor an officer, sir," I reminded him.

"Let's hope I don't get bitten by the larval mites of the trombicula akamushi," Honners said flatly.

Lieutenant Titterton bristled with frustration. "Why can't you speak like a normal human-being, man? What is that in everyday language?"

"It's popularly known as tsutsugamushi."

"Popularly known to whom, Honners—professors of tropical diseases? Name your poison in plain English."

"I thought everyone knew it was scrub typhus. I've seen rats on the island, and this rat carries it."

"Don't tell me you carry it in your handbag?" Lieutenant Titterton jested bitterly.

"You won't say that when you drop dead one morning over your boiled egg and Marmite soldiers."

Everybody laughed except Lieutenant Titterton, who went into command pose. "Now let us forget the whole silly business and get back to bed. It's past midnight already."

Honners moaned deeply. "That's when the crustacea decapoda come out. As many as ten thousand to an acre."

"What do they do—dance round the camp fire? What the devil are they anyway?"

"Land crabs. Big as your head. When they're about to attack humans they stop suddenly and raise one enormous claw in a kind of salute."

"Squeaking Heil Hitler, I suppose. Enough of your banalities, Honners. Everybody back to their bunks."

The crowd dispersed to their tents, treading gingerly through the grass and peering in all directions for weird flora and fauna. For myself I tucked the mosquito-net securely into the blanket all round me to keep out the terrors of the night. To make the darkness more eerie, silent lightning was flickering around the horizon, shooting the strangest shapes onto the tent walls. Honners was still moaning and cursing Lieutenant Titterton, the Marines, islands, and life generally when I eventually fell asleep.

Next morning we experienced the full impact of island diet. The field kitchen drew their rations strictly from tins, right down to rancid butter, bacon and the stringiest corned beef I have ever seen—so stringy that you could unravel it from the huge yellow cans. Everything had to be washed down with boiled bilge-water tea and condensed milk. Bread was what I missed most; biscuits are a very poor substitute indeed, especially at breakfast.

Soon we were reinforcing our rations with three edibles which were in plentiful supply, coconuts, bananas—the smaller plantain variety—and eggs. These latter we learned to procure from a species of pigmy chicken which ran wild over the island. The eggs were white, smaller than pullets, but gratefully received by us. I never tired of the eggs, but an excess of bananas soon palled on the appetite. As for coconuts I could not face one for years afterwards. We learned the native technique of shinning up the palms to cut the nuts, then split the rugby-ball husks on a pointed stick buried in the ground and open the shell with a machete. Any other method was utterly exhausting and disastrous to the nut, as we discovered when Honners lost his temper in the early days and went berserk with a sledge-hammer, shrieking, "Coconut-fudge it is then!"

Two tiny lizards set up home in our tent, catching flies for their dinner. They were delightful creatures, so transparent as they scuttled up the canvas that we could see their bodily organs, even the minute heart beating. These we adopted, naming them Fred and Freda. The seven islands were also named as Piccadilly, Belgravia, Bloomsbury, Mayfair, Soho, Strand and Kensington, our island being Piccadilly. Honners declared such nomenclature to be wet, pathetic, and downright deceitful. In protest he pinned a card over our tent flap which read: Regent Palace Hotel—Full Up.

We discovered that Piccadilly was the largest island of the group, some two miles long by half a mile wide, whereas Soho, the smallest, was no bigger than a football pitch. From his stolen Admiralty chart Honners made the alarming discovery that, while the inside of the lagoon was less than three hundred feet in depth, immediately outside the reef the ocean plummeted to some two thousand fathoms.

"Strewth!" he gasped. "Our little lump of coral is perched up on the summit of a mountain peak like the cock on top of a church steeple."

Our first big assignment was to construct a rough road through the island. This we did by felling trees and laying them side by side to form a wooden track, then covering them with sand and soil. Now we could bring ashore trucks and Matador lorries for the transportation of the guns—coastal guns, Bofors and Oerlikons.

Next, we were required to erect a telephone system, not difficult by using the palms as telegraph poles but not so easy when it came to linking each island to the next by means of submarine cable. The chief trouble was the strong currents which swept between the islands as the great bowl of the lagoon filled and emptied with the tides. Using thirty men to carry the cable on their shoulders we advanced into the water quite steadily until the leaders lost their footings and the cable ended up in a giant semi-circle back to the beach.

On our very first attempt Honners got out of his depth far quicker than his taller companions, to be swept away screaming "Sharks!" finally to disappear round the extremity of our island. A search party was sent to locate him in vain, but three hours later his body was discovered washed up on the beach near the opposite end of the island. He eventually responded to artificial respiration applied by Sergeant Canyon but we never really discovered what happened to him. All he would mumble was "Jonah . . . swallowed by a whale . . . spewed up . . . send me home to mother."

Henceforth Lieutenant Titterton insisted on Honners being secured to a line before entering the water, not so much for his safety, oddly enough, but to force him to go in. "To prevent you being swept away while you are still on dry land," as Lieutenant Titterton phrased it. But the tides proved too strong for us and the operation had to be completed by powerful launches, which were capable of carrying the cable across on a diagonal course against the current. As a result of this business Honners was put on yet another charge for calling cable-laying Drowning by Numbers.

That night when we had finally to abandon our efforts

we slept the sleep of exhaustion, each man temporarily forgetting the mild dysentery we now accepted as inevitable. In the small hours the camp reverberated with the familiar cry of "Berrrrrrr . . . luddy . . . hell!" from our tent. It was like a death scream.

I woke in panic, unable to grasp the situation. There was water everywhere and Honners was shrieking, "Swim for your life! The island's been inundated by the ocean! Take to the boats!"

With that Honners seemed to be swept into me, my bed overturned and the tent collapsed. Then the whole mass of Honners, me, beds and tent began to move along. "We're being swept out to sea!" Honners screamed. "This cursed death-trap of an island must be sliding into the ocean! Take to the boats! Women, children and me first!"

The next thing I remember in the confusion was many hands pulling the tent off me and the sensation that I had been embalmed in mud. Honners was hauled out blackened beyond reognition, dripping with wet debris similar to tea-leaves, and shouting something about the end of the world cometh.

Lieutenant Titterton was trying to direct operations by bawling orders but he found it harder to take command in the dark than in daylight. His troops kept shouting back, "Aye aye, sir," then doing their own thing. Between orders he repeatedly cried, "Curse these two men for camping in a gully! The first heavy downpour of tropical rain and they're swept away like leaves down a drain."

"Why didn't you warn us, sir?" I inquired as soon as I discovered we were not actually in the ocean.

Lieutenant Titterton gave the bitter laugh we knew so well. "I foresaw the danger of course, Pook, but sometimes it is better for inexperienced newcomers to the tropics to learn the hard way."

"But you arrived out here with us," Honners protested. "Let's hope this doesn't give me blackwater fever. That's if I haven't caught it already. I'll bring you a urine sample tomorrow to see for yourself—it's turned navy blue. . . ."

Honners was interrupted by a terrible burst of thunder like a high-level bombing attack. Instinctively we all dropped flat on the ground.

"Take cover, men!" Lieutenant Titterton shouted. "But remember basic precaution number one, not, repeat not, under a tree."

"Not under a tree!" Honners whined. "Where else can you go on an island like this? The whole place is covered with them."

"Do you mean jump in the sea, sir?" I queried.

"I'm not going in the sea for anyone, matey," Honners confirmed. "Anything's better than sharks."

"Of course I don't mean the sea, men. Find a clearing where there are no trees this instant."

"But there isn't one, sir. You didn't tell us to make one."

"First job tomorrow forenoon—make a gigantic clearing," Honners suggested. "Strip the entire island of trees and put up a three-hundred-foot lightning conductor."

"Lie where you are, men. The electrical storm has passed its peak. Despite the violence of the lightning our chances of being struck are a million to one."

"That's how I lost my best friend back in Cudford," Honners groaned. "All they could find was his boots."

"There's a fire burning further along the island, sir," I warned.

Lieutenant Titterton stood up to survey the land. "Just

as I feared, men. Sergeant Canyon, organize all hands for fire picket duty immediately. If that bush fire spreads we may be driven off the island."

"Not me," Honners cried. "I'll stay and be burned. Anything's better than being eaten alive by sharks like I've seen."

"Don't argue, you stupid little coward. At worst we still have boats to take us to an adjoining island."

"Provided they're not all on fire too. . . ."

"Get mobile at once and help quell the conflagration, man."

When we reached the seat of the fire a mighty cheer rose spontaneously from our throats. Lieutenant Titterton arrived breathlessly to the scene as we waded in with brooms and sticks to beat out the flames. Waded in with unnatural zest to flatten the area into the ground like madmen, led by Honners.

Lieutenant Titterton was secretly pleased that at last he had succeeded in motivating his men to such efforts. "The old spirit has been born in the heart of peril, Sergeant Canyon," he exulted. "See what they are capable of when properly officered and inspired. Marvellous! What caused all that cheering, Sergeant?"

"Your tent has been struck, sir. But fortunately they've managed to put it out in double quick time, sir. No danger now."

"Put it out it! They've destroyed it! All my personal possessions!"

"Maybe it was a mistake to fly the Union Jack so high above your tent, sir. Attracted the lightning to it, see."

"Call those thugs off at once, Sergeant. Put Honners on a charge for extinguishing a fire with an axe."

"But how can he be punished further, sir? He's had everything in the book. The only thing left is to stop his shore leave and that don't make sense on this dump of an island."

"I'll think of something, Sergeant. In fact it's been in my mind for some time now. I'll promulgate it tomorrow in Daily Orders. Now fall the men in and march them back to their quarters with Corporal Crood before they start burying the debris."

"Very good, sir."

THREE

Installed on a higher site in a new tent Honners lost no time in setting up shop. In some mysterious way he had obtained a small stock of goodies such as men require on an island, or anywhere else for that matter. There was a seven-pound tin of mixed biscuits, Cadbury's chocolate, various brands of cigarettes and tobacco, cans of beer, shaving-cream, brilliantine, stationery, camera film, even girlie magazines.

Oddly enough, although there was only one of each item on display he never ran short. As each purchase was made so it was replaced when nobody was about, just like magic. When Lieutenant Titterton made inquiries about the sole shop on the island he discovered that Honners had managed to save one of each item when we were stationed in Egypt and was now prepared to sell it for the general good. What Lieutenant Titterton could not fathom was how Honners did such trade, yet still had one of each item left. He had Honners' person, kit and tent searched five times without locating anything untoward, even instigating two spot checks by night, all in vain.

Then he tried the ruse of sending Corporal Crood to purchase the ball of Wright's Coal Tar soap offered for sale. One hour afterwards, Lieutenant Titterton suddenly appeared in the tent. To his disappointment the Wright's Coal Tar soap slot was empty. Honners was dozing on his camp-bed, so Lieutenant Titterton roused him.

"I particularly wanted a ball of Wright's Coal Tar soap for my skin, Honners," he smiled amicably. "I thought you might have one to help me out."

Honners peered in the slot. "Sold it. Oh, I remember;

Corporal Crood bought it an hour ago. Lifebuoy, Palmolive, Sunlight, Lux, Pears—all here."

"I particularly wanted my Wright's, Honners. Perhaps there might be an odd bar under the counter, ha-ha-ha-ha!"

"I only brought one from Cairo. Maybe Puffy will split it with you."

"I do so like my very own bar. Just one for your officer?"

"What about Monkey Brand—Won't Wash Clothes?" Honners said, quoting from the wrapper. "Wright's is out of stock."

Lieutenant Titterton departed in frustrated mood, yet as soon as he was out of sight through the trees a fresh ball of Wright's Coal Tar soap filled the slot. Some folks thought there must be some connection between Selfridges, as Honners called his store, and Honners' job of postman between the island and *Moon of Mandalay* before she sailed away. But Honners continued to do business long after the ship departed and right through our sojourn on the island.

Honners would accept most currencies of the countries we had visited, from Sterling to Egyptian piastres, but all goods cost double their Egyptian prices. We gladly paid the excess for such luxuries, which Honners dubbed Titterton Tax on the goods. Everybody tried to solve the riddle of where Honners obtained his stock and where he hid it but he merely raised his eyes skywards, saying, "What stock? I merely happen to have one of each."

People thought I was in on the racket, but not so. All I knew was that during his rounds Honners seemed to visit the Armaments Depot quite a lot, where he used to spend some time in the vicinity of twelve large wooden crates which were heavily stencilled: DANGER! Defective Ammunition.

Do NOT open.

Another of Honners' enterprises concerned the rum issue. Each forenoon every man was supplied with his ration of neaters, but teetotallers could have threepence in lieu of the spirit. Honners persuaded the teetotallers to draw their rum, then sell it to him for fourpence, or a fivepenny coupon exchangeable at Selfridges Store. With this rum he concocted a drink he called Piccadilly Punch, consisting, according to Honners, of rum, spices, fruit-juices and sugar. Piccadilly Punch retailed at sixpence per enamel mugful and it sold by the bucketful, being so refreshing, delicious and potent.

How, people wondered, did Honners perform the miracle of turning such a limited allowance of rum into such an inexhaustible supply of punch? How, they asked, was it so strong that men became quite tipsy after two mugfuls?

Honners merely smiled superiorly when questioned, saying, "The secret recipe was handed down in my family for generations—so secret that it had to be transmitted by word of mouth and never written down. The chief reason was that it increased our virility."

It certainly increased Honners' capital because he was gradually soaking up every loose note and coin on the island like a giant financial sponge. Our service pay provides a useful yardstick of value for those times. When I joined the Royal Marines I received two shillings per day, but now we were seasoned campaigners drawing hard-liers allowance for living under canvas I was entitled to six shillings and sixpence per day—almost thirty-three pence in our new currency. Jam was still sixpence a pound, cigarettes were fourpence for ten, and a pint of beer cost eightpence.

Some folks with suspicious minds doubted Honners'

story of the ancient family recipe, holding it unlikely that his forbears had the opportunity to help unload medical stores from the *Moon of Mandalay*, as Honners had volunteered to do.

Even Lieutenant Titterton had marvelled at the quantity of stores Honners managed to carry from the invasion-barge on the beach, yet was able to arrive at the tented hospital almost empty-handed. I myself noticed on one such journey that Honners had left the beach staggering under the weight of his burden but when he reached the tented hospital he handed in a small package of bandages.

I had long observed that whatever goods Honners manhandled tended to diminish alarmingly en route. Yet nothing untoward was ever witnessed, nothing was ever recovered, and it was a waste of time searching Honners or his tent. Honners' bland smile of innocence and contentment as he walked about the camp nearly drove Lieutenant Titterton potty. He sought to enlist the aid of Lieutenant Tudor, who had been a hotel detective until the war, but Lieutenant Tudor had no desire to help his brother officer. Nor did he receive much cooperation from the men because the last thing they wanted was Selfridges Store to close down.

Lieutenant Titterton checked the stores' lists time and again, trying to discover what was missing in general, and in particular if a Winchester or carboy of ethyl alcohol had gone astray. But wartime methods of issuing stores in bulk, their widespread distribution around the islands and loss by enemy action finally defeated him. All stores were accounted for, all returns were correct—correct to the last nut and bolt. Because it was physically impossible for Lieutenant Titterton to check everybody's stores personally he appointed a small audit staff to carry out this work, which was delegated to the former accountants, bank clerks and civil servants who were now dressed up as Marines for the duration of the war. Unbeknown to Lieutenant Titterton, Honners and I were both engaged in this audit for him, together with Jack Packer, Ray Smart, Tom Lennox and Vic Stone, all buddies of ours, so the result was one of the tightest ever. The only articles we could report as missing were a small anchor from a pinnace, believed lost during the initial landing, one four pound hammer and one tent-peg.

Honners' unexpected promotion came very early in the morning via Sergeant Canyon. Crusher had a disconcerting habit of breaking news to you when your defences were at their lowest ebb, such as 5.30 a.m., which was half an hour before reveille. A heavy sleeper, Honners had to be shaken all over the bed before he opened his eyes. Directly he perceived it was Sergeant Canyon he moaned, shut his eyes tightly and fell back on the bed crying, "I must be in Hell!"

Sergeant Canyon's rugged face buckled into the nearest he could get to a smile. "I gave you an early shake to bring you good tidings," he announced.

"The Japs have won the war, so we can go home?"

"No, little friend, even better news. First, are you happy in your life with us Bootnecks?"

Honners' face registered extreme bliss. "Paradise! How lucky we are to be living on this tropical Utopia under your tender care. I don't even notice the flies and mosquitoes which plague us as we beguile each treasured hour with merry pastimes. I dread the day we might be compelled to leave and return to the vile world of civilization, edible food, comfort and safety."

"Good, because even better things are in store for you.

Lieutenant Titterton has thought fit to promote his blue-eyed boy in Daily Orders."

Honners opened his eyes at last. "About time too. So far I've put in twenty-seven applications for a Commission and every one turned down. Obviously I have been debarred by my two defects of being slightly short in stature and highly intelligent. According to a book I read my type is ideal officer material."

"What book was that, Honners?"

"The one I'm currently writing called Abolish the Marines. Anyhow, what rank do I start at—a Subbie?"

"Better than that," Sergeant Canyon chuckled. "Captain."

"Captain! Good for Titters. That's one floor above him. Captain the Honourable Lesley Pilkington-Goldberg comes off the tongue pretty sharp. I like it. My compliments to Titters, plus good show and bully for him, what."

"Yes, he promoted you to be Captain of the Heads."

"Captain of the Heads! A lavatory attendant on foreign night-soil! No thanks, you can stuff it."

Sergeant Canyon smiled understandingly and patted Honners' head. "Fair enough, son. You've got freedom of choice in this outfit—that's what this war against the Axis powers is all about, the liberty of the individual. In fact, your charter what protects you is the Articles of War."

"That actually gives me a choice?"

"Sure. You can either do the job or be shot."

I turned over wearily on my camp-bed. "If you're going to shoot him, Sergeant, would you mind doing it after reveille? I'm short of kip."

"Good thing you woke up, Pook, because you're down on Daily Orders as Honners' oppo. Takes two to manhandle

41

them big crap-buckets."

Honners sighed deeply. "To think I was reared in the ambience of Shakespeare, Milton and Keats, yet now I have sunk to this."

"I don't suppose Sergeant Canyon even knows what a Keat is," I observed.

"Don't waste me time on bull," Sergeant Canyon growled. "Let me brief you instead. Now, you may have noticed that our island paradise is surrounded by glorious white beaches, see. Now, I expects you thinks they're made of beautiful white sand, eh?"

"No I don't," Honners replied coldly. "They are composed of finely-powdered skeletons of marine polyps consisting of carbonate of lime, in formations which proliferate between the two 28th parallels of latitude. I do understand the ecology of atolls, you know."

"Is all that guff ruddy coral?"

"It certainly isn't pussers' soap dipped in jam."

"Good. Now, this whole island is made of this 'ere powdered coral, which is porous as 'ell, so we can't risk burying human excrement in it, see."

"So if anything happens to you we must bury you at sea?"

"No, you mouthy little sprogg, we got to ditch all gash in the ocean well to the lee of the island."

"Where is the lee? I haven't seen one. Sounds like a Chinese loo."

"I'll show you where the lee is, Honners. It's the end where the tide flows out to sea. At that point you loads the crap-buckets into the bumboat and dumps them into the 'ogwash not less than half a cable's length from the beach. . . ."

Honners shuddered and held one hand over his mouth. "For pity's sake spare me—at least till after breakfast," he moaned. "On a normal morning it is all I can do to keep down the fried remains of some unfortunate pig that died of old age and was mummified inside a tin. Wash that down with a mug of sweetened mud and I'm all set for the spewers."

Sergeant Canyon grinned delightedly. "Well, get a good breakfast this morning because I want them crap-buckets cleared at eight hundred hours sharp—else it's typhoid and cholera that'll be visiting this tight little dot on the map."

"Sound like his two sisters coming ashore," Honners remarked to me as Sergeant Canyon marched off to shake Marine Ackland to blow reveille.

Honners and I began the worst chore on the island at seven hundred hours by picking up the four full buckets from the latrines and replacing them with empty ones. Each bucket was the size of a dustbin, equipped with handles each side for porterage. Because of the weight Honners had great difficulty lifting his side, and even more difficulty in hoisting the buckets onto the back of an eight-hundred-weight truck. We accomplished it by brute force on my part and violent oaths on his part, then we both sat up front for the drive along our new road of palm-tree logs to the furthest point on the island, which had been named Wopping Old Stairs, apparently to make us think we were still in England.

As we bounced along Honners turned to me and said slowly and deliberately, "Peter . . . you . . . smell . . . like . . . long-range . . . B.O!"

"You smell too, Honners. Everyone smells who does this revolting job. It's all those bananas we eat. . . ."

"Ugh! Shut up!"

With one hand clapped over his mouth Honners stuck his head out of the cab window, then soon withdrew it. "My oath, Peter, it smells worse from the back than it does in here. This truck is surrounded by a mobile cloud of pong."

At Wopping Old Stairs, the lee end of the island, we unloaded the four buckets and carried them as best we could to the bumboat tied up there. Between the stern, where Honners sat, and the bow, where I rowed, was a well that exactly accommodated the four buckets in square formation. Now all we had to do was to scull three hundred yards to the sou'east, jettison the cargo and return to base.

Rowing with the tide was no problem, more a matter of keeping the craft on course. Honners sat astern with a handkerchief over his nose, crouched down in the hope that the smell would pass over him. He was sick over the gunwale once, but I did not inquire whether it was the result of the stench or the waves. Honners was a notoriously poor sailor, declaring that having a bath taxed him to the extreme, and that he had to go easy with the salt-cellar at meals because of his saline allergy. I smiled reassuringly at him, advising him to "Bring it up, mate, because the waves are much worse further out," but he did not seem able to reply.

Using my nautical judgement of distance of three football pitches, I estimated we had gained the right bearing for ditching the gash and shipped oars ready for action. Honners did not exactly leap into the work with gusto. He sat slumped in the stern, eyes tightly shut in a face which was that distressing shade of grey. He mumbled something to the effect that he dared not open his eyes to look upon our slopping cargo, nor release his nose to smell it, so would I perform the necessary chores to jettison the muck, then get him back to the tented-hospital and whip him under an oxygen tent while there was still a chance of his survival.

Whereupon a limited dialogue ensued.

"I can't manage it alone, Honners—the buckets are too heavy and not enough foot-space to handle them."

"Ugh!"

"If you could help me with the first one I'd have more room to manoeuvre the rest."

"Ork!"

"The best way would be to ditch the bucket nearest you."

"Yuk!"

"At least stand up and try, Honners."

"Erk!"

I pulled Honners to his feet and he made some pretence at helping me. Somehow we managed to lift the first bucket onto the gunwale of our little boat, whence I tipped it clumsily into the sea until it emptied. Honners now seemed more concerned with protecting his nose with the handkerchief than getting rid of the stuff, making those shrill noises of disgust which people employ under such circumstances.

It was while we were manhandling the last bucket that an extra high wave rocked the boat so much that both of us staggered about in the well like drunkards. Momentarily I could no longer hold the bucket balanced on the gunwale. Only Honners was supporting it, and as the craft rolled to starboard the bucket went overboard with Honners still clutching the handle. I could not believe my eyes. He went in head first, so that the last I saw of him was the soles of his boots. All that remained was the empty bucket floating near by.

Honners resurfacing was a sight to remember, particularly the size of his eyeballs. He kept shouting, "I'm floating in it!" as though this was an extremely difficult feat that made him very angry.

"Shut your mouth and grab this oar," I advised, trying to collect my wits and remember the treatment for men who fell into sewers. Once I had pulled him to the boat it was quite easy to haul him inboard while he screamed, "Rush me to hospital—I'll need every jab in the book for this lot! I've got multi-typhoid and galloping cholera for a start."

"First thing you need is deodorizing, Honners. You smell to high heaven."

"My oath, Peter, there'll be big trouble over this. Heads will roll, mark my words."

"Don't I know it—we've lost a bucket."

"Damn your buckets, man! I mean endangering my health—probably my life. I'm nothing more or less than a one-man epidemic. Row me back as if you were a robot in a fit."

I searched about me for the oar that I had used to pull Honners in but it had gone. In fact, I could glimpse it floating out to sea. "Not just a bucket, Honners, but an oar too," I confessed.

"Then scull with one oar stuck over the stern, like fishermen do at home. It is a kind of figure-eight movement. Hurry, man."

My attempt at sculling sent our boat round in tiny cirdes, like a floating top. Honners sneered. "Don't ever become a fisherman—you'll sink in your own whirlpool."

"I'm doing my best, Honners. I've never sculled before."

"Obviously. The idea is to propel the boat forward. You position the oar in the sculling-notch at the top of the transom above the stern thwart, then ply it on the same principle as a propeller-blade."

"As you know so much about it why don't you do the sculling?"

"Because I was born to command, not toil. Besides, I'm

an extremely sick man—an extremely sick nobleman, in fact."

After some time experimenting with the oar I managed to get a little way on the craft, but when I checked on our island for direction I cried out in astonishment. Piccadilly had shrunk alarmingly, as though it had drifted away from us towards the horizon. I drew Honners' attention to this optical illusion.

"The reason is, Peter, that we are being swept out to sea on a strong lee tide, or whatever it is they say in the navy when you're at stage one of going off your rocker prior to the approach of a watery grave. Scull like sin and try to regain the island!"

"But I don't seem to make any impression against the current; it's much too powerful. I'll throw this empty bucket over the side and prove it."

When the bucket was floating a few yards off our beam I sculled my hardest, but the bucket remained level with us. "The best thing we can do, Honners, is to attract their attention on Piccadilly so they can come out and tow us in with a launch," I suggested.

"Good thinking, Peter. Let's start right now because they won't see us if we're waving from the other side of the horizon."

I waved the oar high in the air while Honners screamed abuse in the direction of the island. After nearly half an hour of this distress signalling Honners said, "Wonderful, isn't it? Look-out towers everywhere, radar-scanners operational in case the Japs attack, yet they can't spot one of their own boats within gunshot!"

"Maybe they only check on approaching targets, Honners?"

"Don't talk so wet. If the Japanese fleet encircled the

island Titterton wouldn't know it. He'd say it was a tropical mirage."

"Sergeant Canyon reckons there's nothing between us and the South Pole."

"What a source of comfort you are to me in time of desperate trouble, Peter. Now tell me the story of the Titanic."

"But surely Sergeant Canyon will miss us and raise the alarm?"

Honners nodded. "Yes, he'll miss us at tomorrow morning's muster. Then he'll raise the alarm very slowly in the Sergeants' Mess that evening when he's sloshed. He'll say, 'That little slob 'as even wagged my crap-buckets and bumboat.' "

Loyota Atoll finally disappeared over the horizon at six the same evening, so I stopped waving the oar. I was still dazed by that common illusion in vast areas of ocean that we were stationary and the islands had floated off out of sight.

Honners regarded me glumly, as though weighing up how long I would last as a food source when he became compelled to eat me. "Perhaps they'll lay on an air search for us," I suggested, appalled by the enormous empty circle of ocean wherein we were the exact centre.

"And how, pray, will they become airborne for this purpose, may one ask? I personally can scarcely visualize Sergeant Canyon scouring the sea from the back of an albatross. The nearest Allied plane is probably a Swordfish based on Ceylon, with a range several hundred miles short of here. On the other hand you may be prepared to wait for the weekly visit of that Catalina flying-boat which brings us our mail."

"When's that due, Honners?"

"A week yesterday."

"Do you think Crusher will book us for desertion?"

"He certainly won't think we're gone on leave. The one thing he likes about Piccadilly is that nobody can skive off —particularly me."

"Don't you think we should take a bearing or something before the sun sets, Honners?"

My friend sneered. "Hand me my sextant, chronometers, compass and chart, Captain Bligh, then I will. Don't you realize we've got nothing? The only men ever cast adrift with one oar and a crap-bucket. Anyhow, we know exactly where we are. We're here."

Honners drew a cross on the waters with his forefinger, then suddenly jerked his arm inboard. "Carcharodon rondeletti!" he shrieked.

For once I had no difficulty in translating Latin into English because we seemed to be surrounded by a giant maneating shark—all thirty-five feet of him. He swirled lazily round our little craft, so close that Honners and I instinctively hunched up into human bags without arms or legs.

"These pleurotremata have an acute sense of smell," Honners whispered, wide eyed.

"Then directly he's gone we'll get you washed down. We don't want to invite his family over for dinner. If they've got an acute sense of hearing too we'd better shut up. I wouldn't like to offend him. Couldn't we gently push him off with the oar?"

"Excellent idea, Peter. Don't annoy him though."

"Not me, Honners—you."

"Too risky. I smell, remember? You do it. Don't lose

the oar in case you need it later to make a wooden-leg."

"Perhaps a better idea would be to ditch a bucket to distract him, like a red-herring does to foxhounds."

"Good thinking, Peter. I wouldn't waste any time about it either. I don't fancy turning into a red-herring myself."

While the huge grey-brown body was nosing along our port side I lifted one of the two remaining buckets onto the gunwale, gingerly and silently lest it disturb the shark, then gradually lowered the bucket into the sea on the starboard side without splashing. Finally, I quietly pushed the bucket away with the oar in slow-motion.

The stratagem worked because when the shark next circled the boat his attention was diverted by the bucket. Apparently attracted by its smell the shark nudged the base as if trying to turn the bucket over in playful exploration. He stayed with the bucket, and as it drifted away so was the shark drawn from us.

When the crisis was over I requested Honners to plunge into the warm sea and cleanse himself, but for some reason connected with our recent visitor he refused. He would not even scoop water from over the side so, while he watched for fins, I splashed him all over until he was reasonably clean. Then we jettisoned the last bucket and washed the boat as best we could.

"I'm hungry and thirsty," Honners announced when we had completed the task.

"Me too."

"Isn't it marvellous, Peter? In all the books and films the castaways always manage to find some survival gear in the boat or in their pockets. We've got damn-all, not so much as a bent pin for catching fish."

"We don't seem to be on those busy shipping lanes they

talk about, either."

"The only ship we're likely to see is a Jap reconnaissance destroyer looking for target practice."

"I told you ages ago we should have learned to speak Japanese."

"It wouldn't have taken long either. You only need one word—mercy!"

"We don't even know the Japanese for surrender."

"Use mime. Just fall flat on your face with your hands up."

I sat there trying to grasp the fact that we were adrift in so much ocean with no prospect of sighting land. Second only to the Pacific in size, the Indian Ocean seems to fill the globe, stretching right down to the Southern Ocean and the South Pole. Were we able to survive on our present course I figured we would eventually hit Australia.

When the red snooker ball of a sun sank beneath the western horizon I was taken unawares by the rapid onset of the tropical dusk. "It's getting dark," I observed.

Honners yawned. "A natural phenomenon common to most parts of the world, Peter, caused by the revolution of the planet on its axis."

"I don't like it, especially those eerie plops and splashes in the sea all around us. How are we going to get through the night?"

"I don't suppose you believe those terrible tales of ships being overwhelmed by the gargantuan architeuthis princeps?"

"What in hell's that?"

"The giant squid, fifty feet long and capable of pulling a ship under."

"Of course I don't believe it, Honners."

"I do. That's how I lost my cousin, Captain the Honourable Vernon Pilkington-Goldberg, only three years ago. However, that horrible catastrophe happened in the Atlantic so it is unlikely to be our fate in these waters. Besides, to the giant squid we'd be a mere stick of chewing-gum."

"Honners, must you talk about horrors at a time like this?"

"No point in blinking the facts of life, Peter. Our main danger may be the ommastrephes bartrami."

"Tell me quickly or shut up."

"That's the ugly squid which prefers to leap along the surface of the sea than swim. We can probably spot it because I believe it carries phosphorescent lights on its body."

"Honners, I'm begging you to change the subject. I can see phosphorescent light everywhere. Please don't make it worse."

"Very well, Peter, I will change the subject. Are your feet wet?"

"Soaking."

"Exactly. Here in the stern my calves are wet."

"Why is that?

"Because the boat is leaking."

"Oh, Honners, not that! I can't even see it. What time does the moon come up?"

"At this time of the month about 4.30 a.m., so our only light will come from the Milky Way right above us. Observe how Ursa Major is standing on the northern horizon, while to the extreme south we perceive the Southern Cross, proving indeed that we are in the tropical belt south of the equator. Note how Betelgeuse and Rigel, in the constellation of Orion, enable us to pinpoint. . . ."

I was already bailing frantically with cupped hands, rising and stooping like a steam-piston, while Honners continued his survey of the starry firmament above us. "Bail like sin, Honners!" I cried.

"You can't keep that pace up all night," Honners remarked. "Let's get organized into watches, four hours on and four off. That way there will always be one of us working the pumps, so to speak."

"How can anybody sleep when we're sinking in mid-ocean. Bail for your life!"

"Suit yourself, Peter, but you'll find in the long run that you can't beat the Royal Marines' system of watchkeeping, believe me."

As I bailed desperately in the darkness, a steady rhythm of snoring gradually permeated my ears, informing me that Honners had delegated the first watch to me. The most terrible watch of my life.

FOUR

Words cannot really describe the horror of that long night. The combination of fear, hunger, thirst and dread of the unknown was nothing compared with the realization that the only thing between me and death by slow drowning or being eaten alive was the timbers of an old bumboat.

I bailed as best I could, using my stores' issue topee as a bailer, Honners having lost his when he fell overboard, but all the time I wanted to scream with a mixture of despair and terror. I felt alone in some kind of marine jungle, surrounded by the creatures of the night who revealed their presence by plops, splashes and phosphorescence. I actually did cry out on the few occasions when something solid collided with the boat and rocked it, similar to coming alongside a jetty where the impact is softened by a curtain of old rubber tyres.

Although certain I could not sleep under such conditions I began to rouse Honners at midnight by my luminous watch, finally shaking him back to his senses by 12.5. "You've got the middle watch, Honners," I told him, realizing only then that his choice of duty meant that I would have the morning watch at 4 a.m., whereby my stint would be eight hours against his four.

Normally courageous to the point of folly I had lost my British aplomb to the extent that I found myself rousing Honners by his throat. He removed his feet from the thwart and placed them down on the bottom-boards. "My oath, Peter, if anything the water-level is higher than when you took over," he swore indignantly. "What have you been doing on watch—swinging the lead at the risk of my life? Don't you ever think of others?"

"I think about you quite a lot, Honners, and when I stop thinking about you it always surprises me how you're still alive. I didn't stop bailing, man, but the best I could do was to prevent things getting worse. I scooped four hours non-stop. Follow that."

"If you worked as hard as you claim, the results are pretty poor: We're not on the Serpentine in Hyde Park, you know."

"Well, now it's your chance to see if you can do any better. Get splashing, mate."

"One thing's for sure—I couldn't do any worse."

I thought sleep was impossible under the circumstances, yet I dropped off in exhausted slumber despite the discomfort and privations. I woke about two o'clock and took some time to adjust to this dark silent world of warm ocean. Gradually I realized that there was no sound of bailing— yet a steady snore filled the air. I discovered Honners dead to the world in the bow, a satisfied smirk on his face as though he was dreaming of money. I found we were now not so much in a boat as sitting in water surrounded by a wooden rim. Our boat was literally awash. I shook Honners awake by brute force, begging him to help me bail out before we foundered. But I could not locate the topee.

Honners rubbed his eyes sleepily. "You know me, Peter; just a robot when it comes to an emergency. In fact I bailed myself to such a state of exhaustion that the topee eventually flew out of my hands with the water. Then I collapsed in the bow with fatigue, so much so that I must have dozed off for a few seconds in a kind of stroke. I'm my own worst enemy when effort beyond the call of duty is required, so let's hope the strain hasn't damaged my heart permanently. With nobody about to restrain me I just went hell for leather and knocked myself out. I'd better take a long rest before I attempt to do any more graft."

"But we're sinking!"

"Every cloud has a silver lining, Peter. I don't think we can sink any deeper because it's a wooden boat."

"Or a wooden coffin?"

"So long as there's sufficient free-board round us to keep the sharks out we're sitting pretty."

"If we sit here with water up to our necks the sharks won't even know there's a boat underneath us. Bail for your life!"

We bailed as best we could with cupped hands but it seemed to make little difference. When the sun came up from the cloudless horizon there was precious little boat to show for our labours, for only our heads and chests were above water. If we moved too much that portion of the boat submerged entirely, and several small fish, refusing to recognize the difference between boat and ocean, were actually swimming about inside the hull. I kept the oar handy in case we were attacked by larger creatures, and at the back of my mind was a vague idea that if the craft finally sank we could at least use the buoyancy of the oar to keep us afloat.

It was Honners who first spotted the sail on the eastern horizon. "Don't tell me the Royal Navy has run out of fuel," he jested excitedly.

"Looks like an Arab dhow, Honners. Remember all those dhows we saw on the Nile and down the Red Sea?"

"Never. Dhows go up to two hundred tons burden. This one's more like fifty tons. The sail is less triangular and the hull is slimmer and lower. What's more, they're using paddles over both sides. I'd say it's a dhoney, like the ones we sighted off the Maldive Islands when we passed by on the way to Loyota. Wave the oar like a dog's tail."

There was no doubt that we had been sighted because the vessel changed course and was approaching bow on. As she drew nearer we could see that several of the paddlers were boys, yet they paddled in perfect rhythm with the men, working to a strongly-accented rowing chant that drove the boat along with a bow-wave despite the lack of sailing wind.

The captain appeared to be the helmsman. He stood in the sternsheets, using an upright post for support and controlling the tiller with one bare foot. It was he who issued orders to the paddlers and to the crew who handled the sail. Like the rest, he wore only a coloured sarong to the ankles, being naked from the waist up. Round his head was a small turban. Only when the dhoney was closing on us did I realize how tiny these men were. They laughed and called to us, apparently somewhat hysterical to find two white men submerged to their waists in mid-ocean.

With enviable seamanship the helmsman brought the vessel alongside our stricken bumboat, whereupon we were gently hauled on board. A great deal of gasping arose when they discovered how long I was, over six feet, but it was Honners who seemed to hold them spellbound. They marvelled at the fact that, whereas I was a giant, Honners was shorter than they were. They peered closely at his retroussé nose, obviously restrained only by their natural courtesy from feeling its curve with their fingers. Honners' ginger hair brought cries of wonderment from their lips as they crowded round him so closely to inspect it and sniff it.

Honners turned to me smilingly. "Observe, Peter, how these natives, unhindered by the veneer of modern civilization, can still smell the blood royal in my veins."

"I don't think it's the blood royal they're smelling,

Honners, just the hangover from when you fell in the muck yesterday."

"Rubbish. They probably think I'm some kind of god who has risen from the deep. The main thing is that at least we're safe. The next thing to do is to establish communication. Once I've discovered which language family their lingo derives from I shall be able to chat quite freely."

It was remarkable how Honners had employed this method to establish communication in various parts of the world, only to discover that the inhabitants under analysis were unable to speak or comprehend their own language. As usual when east of the Mediterranean Honners' opening gambit was, "Hullo dere, man," delivered in a deep bass as though he was about to sing Old Man River. Our hosts laughed delightedly, and, imitating Honners, replied, "Hoderman," over and over again until the cry was taken up right round the dhoney.

"Who dis people?" Honners demanded, indicating the crew with his hand.

"Hoodispeepall?" they echoed, sweeping the air with their right hands as Honners had done and striving to emulate his deep tone.

"What lingo you speak den?" Honners boomed irritably.

"Wottingo oospikden?" chorused the crew.

"Sounds as though I'm leading the prayers, Peter. I'll try Arabic, Sinhalese, Tamil and Malay for 'Do you understand me?' "

The audience laughed uproariously at Honners' oration, as though he was telling jokes on a stage. This upset Honners so much that he shouted, "Listen, idiots!"

"Lissenidits!" they shrieked delightedly. "Lissenidits!"

"Listen, idiots—don't try and take the mick out of me!"

Honners pointed by the sun to the north-west horizon. "Me heap big white chief from mighty land ober dere!"

As one man the natives cried, "Lissenidits!" and pointed to the same horizon with their outstretched arms and forefingers, as if giving some kind of tribal salute. We did not realize at the time how many races do not point with the forefinger, using the extended hand with thumb laid across palm instead. Honners was not to live this down because in future these islanders invariably greeted him with, "Lissenidits!" followed by the forefinger salute to the north-west, similar to the Moslem custom of facing the compass direction of Mecca for their daily prayers.

In fact, we soon discovered that our new friends were not Moslems, but they had got it into their heads that Honners was somebody quite unique in their experience. Honners himself was confident that he had been taken for a long dead hero who had returned to life by some miracle of the sea, while I suspected they regarded him as a freak of nature. I kept this opinion strictly to myself, especially when we were disembarked upon their island and the entire population awaiting the dhoney on the beach sighted Honners and fled screaming to disappear among the trees.

I observed our captain run inland, probably to brief his headman of the village, while the crew set about beaching the dhoney. It was fascinating to watch how they did it. Two boys placed wooden rollers under the prow to engage the keel, while the rest of the crew lined up either side of the vessel. Then a vigorous chant was sung, and at the end of each phrase the crew jerked the boat forward about three inches. This series of tiny movements over a long period enabled such small people to haul the big heavy dhoney well clear of the water.

The skipper had obviously done his homework thoroughly on the headman, who approached us very slowly before pointing to the horizon and crying, "Lissenidits!"

"You impertinent old midget!" Honners gasped. "I happen to be the Honourable Lesley Pilkington-Goldberg of Cudford Hall. . . ."

"Return the greeting, Honners," I advised. "They think it's your personal salute."

"Why should I?"

"Because we're lost and they're not. When in Rome do as Rome does."

"When in Rome! Of all the damned puerile expressions to trot out on this two-by-four sandbank they call an island!"

Nevertheless, Honners had the sense to return the salutation, whereupon the headman conducted us through the trees to a tiny village. The huts were constructed of woven palm leaves supported by frameworks of bamboo, so skilfully and neatly done as to make a pleasing picture to the eye. What interested me most right now was the food being set out on the ground in front of the headman's hut by men and boys. It seemed that the women had fled for the time being, though I often caught sight of shy eyes peering from behind huts and trees to glimpse the little white man with the ginger hair and curved nose.

We were invited to sit round the feast area, but I noticed that the headman had placed Honners at the head of the table, so to speak, on a fat cushion. Much of the delicious food I failed to identify but that did not prevent our enjoying it. Dishes familiar to me were sweet potatoes, millet, chillis, chupatties, fried plantains, goat meat, various fish and shellfish dishes from crabs to prawns, and chicken. The many fruits included guavas, melons and my favourite papaya or pawpaw.

"De . . . licious!" I remarked to Honners, mouth full.

He licked his fingers with closed eyes. "Especially as you seem to have a partiality for grilled rump snake, Peter."

"Snake!"

"Grilled rump snake is succulent, as you have just discovered. Why you make such a fuss after eating fried spider beats me."

"Spider! Don't tell me I've eaten spider!"

"Of course. Second course, as a matter of fact. It is similar to the South American mygale—has a leg-span of over twelve inches, spins a web like a tennis-net and eats birds. Piquant, as we sigh in the best gourmet circles over such a delicacy."

"Ugh!"

"I do wish you were more cosmopolitan, Peter, and less parochial in your tastes. It lets me down badly in company. You seemed to enjoy the first course, bummalo."

"Well, I recognized that as Bombay duck, near enough."

"So, if you like dried scopelidae, which it is, why not dried cephalopoda?"

"What on earth's that, Honners?"

"Octopus!"

"I've actually eaten octopus!"

"Heavens, man, these folk have put on a big tamasha in my honour so they've pulled all the stops out. You should feel flattered."

"I don't. I feel sick."

"What! After they've gone to the trouble to serve us fried bees, toasted termites and grilled grasshoppers."

"I thought they were chips."

"Chips, he says! Save me from the proletariat. You'll

want tea and buns next. You wouldn't get delicacies like these at the Savoy, man. Here, have some nuts and shut up."

"Are they from some unfortunate animal?"

"Cashew-nuts from the anacardium occidentale—that's a tree if you're still worried about your stomach. Think of the muck we ate on Piccadilly Island and be thankful."

Honners had at last established communication with the headman by a combination of oaths, mime and drawing on the sandy floor. There was some confusion in Honners' mind as to whether this island was called Komaddu, or the word Komaddu meant Honners' foot. He and the headman were engaged in a long exchange on the matter.

Honners pointed once more downward to the ground. "Dis place Komaddu den," he boomed in the pidgin English of the early movies.

"Komaddu," the headman confirmed, also pointing downward. Then he picked up Honners' bare foot, saying "Komaddu."

The headman solved the mystery for us by drawing round Honners' foot in the sand, then pointing all round the island.

"They can smell your feet all over the island," I suggested.

"No, idiot. The shape of this island resembles a human foot, so Komaddu means Foot Island. The chief charlie here seems to think I'm some kind of god—far-fetched but quite understandable—so we've been assigned the finest hut on the Mali, furthest from the muck-heap. He reckons you are my giant bodyguard, chuprassi and general dogs-body, so you can come too."

"Much thanks, O mighty Shortarse the Bold."

Arriving at the hut we were surprised to discover our bumboat parked outside, decked with flowers. Next day two of our buckets appeared, similarly decorated, which the islanders treated with the veneration due to sacred icons. Far from pleased, Honners indicated by mime that these relics were far too precious to stand there and must be returned to the sea whence they had come. It was an unforgettable sight to see Honners bowing down before a crap-bucket, as part of the mime, then indicating the ocean.

As we lay on our blanket beds during the second night in the village I drew Honners' attention to the fact that several of the islanders possessed an extra thumb, while others had a surplus little finger. These were thin appendages which seemed to be quite useless.

"One of the disadvantages of an isolated community, Peter," he replied airily. "Such mutations arise from breeding too closely, as is inevitable here. If my old family quack, Butcher Budden, were with us he'd apply a quick local anaesthetic to the hand and whip those redundant digits off like warts. That's why I never complained to him about things such as a sore arm—I didn't want to end up like Nelson."

"You don't seem very anxious to leave the island, Honners."

He laughed. "Leave? Just call me king and forget it. Isn't this better than our existence under Crusher Canyon—nature's answer to happiness?"

"But I feel in a way that we're deserters."

"This is the best form of desertion—we couldn't help it. We were swept away whilst on active service fighting for King and country, engaged upon a hazardous mission beyond the call of duty. Missing, believed drowned."

"What's so good about that?"

"Because I read it as missing, believed safe. No more war for you and me, chum. Nobody knows we're here. I'm obviously the big white Raj, and we've both got big eats with no graft. That supper tonight was out of this world."

"I ate it but have you any idea what it was?"

Honners smacked his lips. "We had turtle soup for starters, then dried fish-blood fritters for hors-d'oeuvre. The main course was braised bats in toddy sauce, then came the pud of. . . . "

"Stop, Honners! Can we come to an arrangement that any food talk is taboo between us? I've been sick twice already."

Because of the unfamiliar menu I was not eating as much as Honners, but it was noticeable how the headman, Honners had christened him Tiddler, plied my friend with food beyond our standards of hospitality, while neglecting my own platter completely. This occurred so regularly that a ridiculous presentiment entered my head that Honners was being fattened up for Christmas, so to speak. Ever the little gourmand, Honners revelled in the attention paid him and seldom refused the second, third, even fourth helpings heaped on his platter, so that he left each meal a belching barrel who must sleep off such excess. In addition, trays of tempting delicacies were placed by his bed each evening lest he suffer from night starvation. By the end of the week Honers had developed a pot-belly he could not conceal.

"Naturally they treat me as a sultan, Peter," he said when I commented on his new shape. "My role in life is to rule the masses and be a symbol of regal power."

"That's OK if the symbol of regal power is supposed to be pear-shaped."

Honners helped himself to a kind of coconut-fudge. "As a matter of fact, Peter, Tiddler has already indicated that if anyone offends royal me, the culprit is to be put in the cage."

The cage was the local jail. It consisted of a bamboo

cage some five feet square, which, when housing an offender, was hauled up on a rope to the top of a palm-tree in the village centre for all to see. Sometimes I speculated how Honners would not mind overmuch if I was inside it.

The headman had already made it plain to Honners that he could have a girlfriend on tap should he so desire. Honners beamed, replying in the affirmative with such basic mime that the headman had suffered mild hysterics. To be fair, this happened to all the islanders whenever Honners showed off—which was pretty often. The children rolled on the ground holding their stomachs and crying helplessly at Honners' simple comedy—or even at Honners being serious. A typical example was the occasion when he wanted a coconut, and showed his wish by embracing the trunk of a great tree, then pretending to lift it out of the ground.

That same evening the headman brought a kind of Miss World line-up to the hut for Honners to choose. There were ten girls in all, but their looks put Honners in an extremely embarrassing position. Whereas the men were short and lean, the girls were short and plump, and their standards of beauty had little connection with ours.

"Go ahead, lover boy, and pick your chick," I chided him.

Honners, who previously had been brought up on a diet of Hollywood movies wherein tropical islands were teeming with gorgeous hula-girls, was appalled. "I'm looking for a bride, not a nightmare," he replied wretchedly. "How do you kiss a girl who's wearing a bone through her nose?"

"When in Rome. . . ."

"For the first time in my life I prefer the fellows."

"But these are the belles of Komaddu, Honners. You

should see the plain ones. Besides, if you don't choose your sweetie it'll upset the old man something cruel. They'll consider it an insult."

"Then why the devil don't you pick one for yourself? With a pan like yours you should be flattered—the man who makes every woman seem as beautiful as Helen of Troy."

"Don't be childish, Honners. They haven't offered me a bride because I'm not fat enough. The way you're spreading you'll soon be a bigamist. Select one of the lovelies and do your duty for England."

When Honners had recovered from the shock and disappointment, he seemed to have found a solution to the impasse. He walked up and down the line of girls, leering at each one while they giggled shyly and trod on their own toes in embarrassment.

"It's going to be one of those difficult marriages, Peter," he remarked. "Good home-cooking but not a lot of conversation. What have we got in common?"

"Your weight problems," I suggested.

Completing his inspection, Honners told me to stand beside the girls. Then he indicated by mime to the headman that he required a wife as tall as me. "That's solved it, Peter," he nodded.

Misunderstanding Honners' mime, the headman ordered a bench to be brought for the girls to stand on, bringing them to the required height. Yet it was obvious from the mood of the tribe that Honners could not evade his responsibilities by trickery. They began chanting and clapping in unison, as if this encouragement would continue until he had selected a village maiden.

I sensed the atmosphere very strongly. "Please the tribe and choose a bride—then we can all go to bed," I advised.

"Give me a number," Honners snapped.

"Lucky seven."

"I asked for a number, not superstitious optimism."

Nevertheless, Honners counted along the line, then pointed to the seventh girl. A tremendous roar of approval arose from the crowd, as they extended their forefingers to the sky and shouted, "Lissenidit!"

There followed a kind of instant marriage service, admirable in its simplicity. The headman grasped Honners and the girl by the right wrists, swung their arms round in a complete circle, then brought their hands together with a slap, all the time reciting a formula we could not understand.

"You're spliced, Honners," I informed him, "Congratulations, may you always be happy together and have many children."

Honners snorted. "Whose side are you on, Peter?"

"Yours of course. I always said the Pilkington-Goldbergs needed new blood to keep the line healthy."

"Yes—healthy and white. This is merely a marriage of convenience. Can you imagine me turning up at The Hall pushing a pram and saying, 'Greetings, pater. I want you to meet my son, an extremely sunburnt eleventh earl who will carry on the title.' He'd go potty and throw himself into the moat."

Like most events on the island, the ceremony was the excuse for general feasting. The celebration banquet started at nine that same evening, and at midnight we were still gorging. Honners was now waited upon by his spouse, whose name was Mooza as closely as I can spell it phonetically. She tended Honners so effectively that he lay on the cushion bloated and belching, yet every time he opened his mouth to protest she neatly popped more delicacies into it. By one o'clock Honners gave up trying to talk to me because his mouth became so full in the process. The last thing I remember him uttering was, "She must think she's a feeding machine, Peter. I can hardly breathe. Perhaps it's calorie saturation. . . ."

As Mooza and I helped him back to our hut there was little room in my mind for doubt now. Not only were the islanders fattening him up for reasons best known to themselves but also they could no longer conceal their delight in his rounded stomach, even daring to stroke it with their fingers like one might do to a ripe peach. A ridiculous feeling gripped me that our hut was a hive containing the queen bee. Then an even stranger thought entered my mind —was it possible that these small delightful people were cannibals? I had read that cannibalism still existed in various parts of the world, so could it be that the practice was common on this remote island? Maybe, I reflected, this isolated community regarded Honners as we of the West regarded caviare—a rare delicacy that seldom came their way. Could it be that Honners would go down in Royal Marine history as the first man to go into battle and be eaten?

"Good-night, Fatty," I said sadly, trying hard not to see Honners as a packed lunch in my mind's eye.

"Good-ni'. . . ." Once again Honners received a mouthful of coconut-fudge from his adoring Mooza as he lay flat on his back with closed lids.

The night plays strange tricks on one's imagination, for I had to endure a horrible dream in which the whole tribe was seated round a fire. Slowly turning on a spit above the flames was Honners—well-browned and smelling delicious.

FIVE

It was one of those nightmares that are so realistic that next day you are positive the events really happened. So I was quite surprised to discover Honners still alive and uncooked. I even went so far as to smell his skin and check his hair for burns. In the light of day my fears seemed ridiculous and I told Honners so.

"I was so worried about you being fattened up for Christmas that last night I had the most horrific dream," I explained frankly. "You were being roasted on a spit while Tiddler basted you. There was that gloriously yummy smell of Sunday dinner, and everybody was smacking their lips. Even I felt hungry."

"Oh good," Honners replied coldly as Mooza departed to fetch breakfast, or chota hazri as we preferred to call it. "Sounds more like wishful thinking to me."

"Of course it was stupid, yet these people may be cannibals."

"My people are loyal subjects, Peter—they do not desire to eat their Raj for whom they have waited so long."

"Then why are you being stuffed like a pre-christmas turkey?"

"That is the way my people demonstrate their joy at my presence."

"Supposing—just supposing—they were cannibals long ago and something about you has revived their interest in that practice. We'd be in the soup."

"An unfortunate choice of metaphor, Peter, but the notion is absolutely preposterous. They adore me."

"There would be no escape, Honners. You can't hide on a tiny island and you can't get off it. One day you could disappear and their menu would be meat-balls all round, or Honners-and-rice curry."

Honners waved me to be silent. "Don't be disgusting, Peter. Your trouble is too many movies and novels. It's gone to your head. Forget the whole business and enjoy yourself."

Despite Honners' confidence I sensed he was slightly worried underneath the bravado, so I figured this was the time to show him what true friendship meant. I placed my hand reassuringly on his shoulder. "We've been through a lot together, chum, and I'll stand by you as I always have done in the past. I want you to know this, that no matter how tough the going or how much pressure they put on me, no man will ever force me to eat any of you, not so much as one little toe."

Honners gave me a sickly smile. "What a comfort you are to me in time of trouble, Peter. Nice to know that one's best friend is a vegetarian and won't be banging the table impatiently with his knife and fork at the ready."

"What's more, I'll claim I'm a Buddhist, so I'm not allowed to kill any living creature, let alone eat my friends. I thought you should know that in case anything awful happens. It helps when the heat's on if you can be sure that your best mate doesn't fancy you."

"Shut *up*!"

"Well, I don't want to see you jump from the frying-pan into the fire."

"Silence, pig!"

For several days the islanders manifested an unusual interest in the sun, often looking up at it quickly around the hour of midday. The focus of this interest seemed to be the well in the centre of the village. It was obviously of some antiquity judging by the stone parapet which measured about four feet across the mouth. The well must have been dug with considerable skill for it was perfectly circular and so vertical that a plumb-line must have been used.

Two things became clear. The first was that the villagers made a habit of peering down the well at noon, and the second was that when they met Honners they smiled strangely and rolled their eyeballs suggestively. The children were even more direct, rubbing their little stomachs and smacking their lips, then shrieking with a kind of glee that was half mirth and half embarrassment. There was some link between the well and Honners that I tried to fathom.

Then a third factor began to take shape. Near the well a great fire of timber was being prepared, and over the timber the islanders were constructing an elaborate spit large enough to roast a goat. I advised Honners not to look down the well in case it was some kind of trap, but he did so at the first opportunity. Then he beckoned to me to follow suit.

As we walked away from the well I commented, "I can see the connection between you and the roasting-spit, Honners, but the well beats me. Surely they don't intend to drown you first, then give you the cordon bleu routine over the fire?"

"For heaven's sake stop being so crude, Peter. You make things far worse than they are."

"They can only get worse when it happens, chum," I replied sorrowfully.

"What did you notice about the well?"

"Nothing really, except that it went straight down and was very deep. I recall from school that if they throw you down it and you take one second to hit the water it means that the well is thirty-two feet deep. What did old Leigh call it in our physics lessons—Newton's Second Law of Motion?"

"Thanks. Didn't you notice the sun reflected in the water at the bottom?"

"I suppose I did now you mention it. What does that mean?"

"It means that we're in dead trouble."

"Like if you take three seconds to hit the water you'll know that you've plunged exactly one hundred and twenty-eight feet to your death?"

Honners winced. "Listen, Peter. When the Ancient Egyptians tried to measure the distance to the sun they needed a true right-angle for part of the trigonometry involved. They obtained it by sinking a vertical well-shaft, so that when the sun was reflected in the water at the bottom they knew they had got the sun at exactly ninety degrees."

"Why should these islanders want to measure that?"

"They don't—they are using the same method to discover when the sun is directly overhead. Bang on the equator that happens about September 21st, but we're south of the equator so it happens a bit later. They know that when the sun is reflected right in the centre of the water at the bottom of the well that's midday and their mid-summer."

"How does that affect you and me, Honners?"

"Because that day must be a big one for them, rather like we celebrate Christmas on the day when the sun is furthest from us, and is, in fact, overhead at the Tropic of Capricorn. Thus a day of holiday and revelry."

"And feasting," I reminded him. "Can you estimate how long you've got before it's Honners-in?"

"What do you mean by Honners-in?"

"Honners-in tomato sauce, like herrings-in."

Honners scowled. "I don't know what your game is, Peter, unless you're trying to do the impossible—undermine the morale of a Pilkington-Goldberg, but I must warn you that there's a nasty shock coming your way which may have escaped your notice."

"What kind of a shock, Honners? You mean they'll torture me till I'm forced to . . . well . . . become a cannibal too?"

"I'll show you directly I have made a calculation. You see, the reflection of the sun in the well today is eccentric, that is, slightly off centre in the circle of water. Each day as the summer solstice approaches, the sun's reflection will pass closer and closer to the centre each midday until it's bang on target. That will be the big eats day."

"How long have you got then, old pal of my childhood?"

"I figure between three and four days at the most."

"I shall miss you, Honners. Everybody says what a scab you are but I don't listen to gossip—I like you, if no one else does, I told Sergeant Canyon that no man is all bad. Dig deep enough, I said, and you'll find a redeeming feature."

"What did he say to that, Peter?"

"He said I must be some digger, so name one."

"Then you let him have it, eh?"

"Not really. I couldn't think of anything to say off the cuff. All your redeeming features went out of my head."

Honners sniffed and looked at me down his nose. "That's the trouble with the working classes, they behold a Tintoretto and see a railway poster. Anyhow, just to wipe the smirk off your pan take a gander at the fire preparations, then tell me if you feel like joining in a tribal waltz for rain."

I turned round from the well to check on the ominous

roasting-spit, only to perceive that another spit was in course of erection—almost double the length of the original one. Normally fearless in the face of overwhelming odds, I was caught off guard by the spectacle, losing my customary imperturbality to the extent of a scream of terror. I found myself sitting on the wall of the well, having apparently lost the use of my legs, neither could I speak nor stop trembling. Apart from these small symptoms of surprise I did not bat an eyelid.

"You took it like a man," Honners commended me. "You didn't even faint. I expect you're thinking right now what have we to fear against eight hundred little fellows armed only with old-fashioned machetes and fishing-spears? Once we've defeated them in unequal combat we'll make a dash for freedom in the shark-infested ocean and swim over the horizon to safety. Why don't we burst spontaneously into a victory song on the spot to make the foe tremble?"

"Don't joke, Honners. Get me off this cursed island fast."

"There will be a small prize for finding the correct solution to that one—such as every penny I have in the bank and Cudford Hall thrown in. Now the first thing you have to do is stop panicking like a jelly on a speedboat. Try to remember you're a Bootneck."

"I want to stay a Bootneck too. At least if you get killed in action they can bury you. I don't fancy ending up down Whitehall as the Unknown Thigh Bone."

"You didn't worry so much when there was only one roasting-spit."

"But they're fattening you up, not me, Honners."

"Because you're too big already—they don't want to be sick."

"I know what we'll do. We'll hide. Take some grub

with us and live rough up the end of the island. Anything's better than being a sitting duck in the village. We might be able to get away in one of their small boats, or we could build a raft."

Honners actually laughed aloud. "Hide! On this place? It would be like hiding from a bear inside his cave. They even know if you pick a berry."

Nevertheless, Honners did help me to store food secretly during the two days that followed. Each noon we checked the sun in the well and how far the feast preparations had progressed. When the natives met us now they made little effort to conceal their delight, actually pointing to the spits and rubbing their stomachs in elaborate mime. On the fourth day Honners declared that our time had run out and we must flee, for everything seemed to be working up as if it was the eve of the big day.

Leaving Mooza in the deep sleep of childhood we stole forth at midnight with our emergency rations wrapped in palm-leaves and walked to what Honners called the heel of the island, the fall end which was little used by the villagers. All was quiet and seemingly our retreat was unobserved. Being Master of Hounds with Cudford Hunt, Honners decided we must make for the beach, then walk through the shallow waters until we reached our destination lest the islanders might track us by smell.

Skirting the beach in this fashion we reached the heel of the island soon after one o'clock by my watch, as Honners announced, "Well that's it, matey—we've run out of land."

"Ugh!" I exclaimed, partly because I was beginning to feel like a walking meal and partly because the night shift of nature's fauna was very much in evidence. Unidentifiable creatures scampered across our path and floppy things collided lightly with our faces. The night chorus of crickets, frogs and other nocturnal choristers was indescribably loud in the still air, while another category, such as bats, seemed to be constantly bickering with their neighbours and throwing one another out of bed, to land on me.

"Shall we go back, Honners?" I inquired, shaking a long thin crawler off my bare leg. "I think we've walked into an insect reservation of six-inch earwigs."

"Never. We planned this and we'll stick to it even if it kills us."

I failed to see much merit in his argument, which smacked of Hobson's choice at its worst. I was thinking more along the lines of better the devil you know than the one you don't.

"Start searching for timber so we can build a raft," Honners commanded in a tone of voice that implied we were surrounded by planks cut to the right length if only I would use my eyes and collect them.

In the darkness I groped for wood, picking up at least three sticks that suddenly came to life and jerked from my grasp. I didn't collect any more. Instead, I said to Honners, "We can't start building a raft till the moon rises. When's that?"

"Tomorrow afternoon—it's just set. Don't waste time, Peter, get your timber together in a pile."

"Every bit of wood I collect runs off."

"Timber I said, not fauna. Go for the long branches that we can plait together, man."

"Plait a raft! What about the sharks, Honners?"

"Hurry, Peter. There's no time to lay down the keel for an ocean cruiser I would have to fashion with my penknife. Get cracking and deliver the goods before dawn. That's when they'll come searching for us. I want to be over the horizon by sunrise."

"On a plaited raft?" I just could not absorb the enormity of Honners' plan, which sounded as though he was under the impression that we were groping about for sufficient twigs to build a powerboat. "Which horizon, Honners?"

"Any horizon. The horizon we drift over. Any horizon that's not connected with this island. That way at least we stand a chance of being picked up by somebody who doesn't want us for the Sunday joint."

I chose my wood by gingerly testing it with my foot to ensure it was dead and not liable to terrify me out of my wits by shooting off, or, as in one case, flying up in the air on wings. But at least it helped to take my mind off the eerie night, so I collected all the branches I could find in the area.

Not until 3 a.m did I realize I had lost contact with Honners. The sense of loneliness on top of fear was horrible. At first I called softly without success, but after ten minutes I was shouting his name unashamedly through the forest, desperate to locate him for human companionship. At 3.30 I could hardly believe my ears, for coming from afar through the tropical night was a steady snore. I tracked onto this sound like radar and located Honners fast asleep in a clearing. Seized with temper and terror I shook him awake by the throat, actually banging his head on the grass. While I was wondering if I should do the job properly and kill him he woke up and whined, "I dropped in my tracks, Peter, completely bushed. Collecting so much timber put paid to me; could have had a stroke."

"Show me this timber-yard before I murder you, you miserable little double-crosser."

Honners waved a hand vaguely in the direction of the beach. "All stacked ready for construction, Peter," he gasped. "Where's your lot?"

"How the devil do I know? I've been wandering round in the darkness for the last half-hour trying to find you."

"Don't say you've lost yours in our hour of need, Peter?"

"If you can find yours I can find mine. It'll soon be sunrise so there's enough light to see by now. Your great pyramid of timber should stand out like a landmark against the eastern sky. Get mobile, bold forester."

We failed to locate Honners' huge collection of wood which he claimed had cost him so dear, but when we discovered mine he moaned, "Really, Peter, this is just not good enough. Surely in an emergency like this you could have made some effort; this little bundle wouldn't support a toad."

"Added to your stack it would have supported both me and the toad—but the toad skived off and kipped down for the night."

"I object most strongly to this attitude you have that I do everything, right from the drawing-board to the finished article. Hey-ho, beggars can't be choosers so let's cut our boat according to our cloth. Oh, if only you would pull your weight as an equal partner instead of pimping on me."

I could have wept with frustration as Honners began the hopeless task of trying to weave the branches together in the shape of a raft some six feet square, resembling a makeshift sieve. When he launched it in the sea by lying across it and paddling with his hands it disintegrated so quickly that Honners sank beneath a kind of giant wreath.

It was when Honners stood up in his depth that I realized how events had affected my nerves in the shape of a sea mirage. There on top of Honners' head was an invasion-barge planing the sea towards us, but I was distracted from the delusion by Honners, who pointed along the beach and shouted. "There's the search party coming to recapture us The game's up, Peter!"

Far along the white beach I perceived dozens of islanders running along the sands, waving and shouting. Then I heard Honners cry, "Look, Peter—one of our invasion-barges! They've spotted us! Surely that's Lieutenant Gull waving his arms up for'ard. Swim for your life! It's our only chance!"

Dazedly I tried to take in the situation, fearful of sharks —yet even more terrified of capture. But the natives were so close as they sprinted along the shore that I followed Honners into the sea and struck out for the rescue boat. Honners was shrieking, "Thrash your legs to keep the sharks off!" whereupon I sent up a veritable gusher of water and windmilled my arms in a desperate crawl that drove me ahead of Honners. He was a poor swimmer at the best of times but now he had turned into a human paddle-boat, bashing the water with arms and legs, sending up a huge quantity of spray and even more foul language. It was as though he had gone off his rocker and was throwing a fit in which he imagined he was killing the ocean.

Behind me I glimpsed the islanders as they reached the place where we had been standing only minutes earlier, still waving and shouting to us. Ahead, the invasion-barge was rapidly approaching, so close now that I could hear Lieutenant Tudor issuing orders. As the craft swung round to starboard to present her beam to us boarding-nets were already in position, lifebelts were cast off and the whole operation of rescue began. The best part of it, from our point of view, was the eight Marines who dived overboard with lifelines on the order given by Lieutenant Tudor, four of whom swam to Honners—who was now emulating the dolphin in that he was leaping in and out of the water but lacking the dolphin's ability to progress forward.

Within minutes we were safely on board the invasion barge. I felt pretty good now the danger was over, but Honners' supreme exertions to escape had taken its toll and he lay on the deck in conventional corpse pose, apparently drowned. Lieutenant Gull hauled him upside-down by his legs while Lieutenant Tudor squeezed his stomach to eject the salt-water like emptying a bottle.

"Cannibals!" Honners moaned as soon as he could speak.

Seeing Lieutenant Tudor's puzzled expression I saluted smartly to let him see the Royals don't lose their composure under fire. "Thank God you came in the nick of time, sir," I barked in the clipped tones essential to military conversation. "Another five minutes and the pair of us would have been roasted alive."

"By whom, Pook?" Lieutenant Tudor inquired.

"By those natives sir. We've managed to escape solely because we foresaw the danger and decamped under cover of darkness."

Honners sat up. "I calculated this was the day of reckoning, so characteristically I devised a plan to save both Pook and myself. By taking command of the situation, guiding Pook and employing split-second timing I managed to get both of us off the enemy beach-head."

"How remarkable," Lieutenant Tudor observed quietly.

"Anybody would have done the same in my shoes. All they required was luck, brains, foresight and the determination to carry out the plan no matter what the cost. I don't seek reward, promotion or medals—I merely did what came naturally to me in the course of duty."

"Splendid, Honners," Lieutenant Tudor said absent-mindedly as he looked over his shoulder. "Hard a-port there and tie up fore-and-aft."

I followed Lieutenant Tudor's gaze and was astonished to see how we had landed on the beach at the toe of the island. Lieutenant Gull was actually waving to the headman of the village and beckoning him to come aboard through the shallow water. When Honners saw what was happening he screamed, "Get the hell out of here! They'll murder the lot of us!"

Lieutenant Tudor raised an eyebrow. "These are the most friendly and gentle people on the face of the globe, Honners. That's why we're here."

"I thought you came to rescue Peter and me, not hand us back for sausage meat."

"Calm down and don't talk rubbish as if you're delirious. You and Pook were written off ages ago. Nobody imagined you could survive in a rotting bumboat. As we rounded Haipa Island we happened to spot you on the beach."

"Wrote us off! Life sure is cheap in the Marines. Back home we took more care of our blessed cat."

"As far as I'm concerned you're officially dead, pre-sumed drowned."

"Then why are you here?"

Lieutenant Tudor smiled. "To deliver the goods. When the area was reconnoitred last year as a possible base for the fleet we discovered how helpful and friendly these little people were, so we decided to consolidate such an advantage by making them a goodwill present."

"Sounds like the present was me."

"The interpreter we're carrying on board right now, Sharif Khan, explained that there are no animals on Haipa Island or any others in this part of the Indian Ocean because there is no grazing ground for them. Therefore their greatest need is meat."

"That's why they intended eating me."

"Nonsense, Honners!—Your head is stuffed with silly films and books. They wouldn't eat you if they were starving. Who would? They wanted meat to celebrate the annual feast of their sea god, Shuma, so we brought along two carcasses from stores—one bullock and one sheep. That's why they're so excited."

Honners sneered. "Go tell that to the Marines."

"But it would account for the two roasting-spits of different sizes," I pointed out.

"We're unloading the gifts right now because they start their big fry-up at sundown."

"But they were actually fattening me for slaughter," Honners persisted. "They as good as said that I was the main course."

"That I fail to understand," Lieutenant Tudor admitted. "I'll ask Sharif Khan to find out why they fancied you when nobody else does. Wait here till I return."

"I certainly shan't be rushing ashore to see the sights," Honners confirmed. "I don't believe a word of it."

Lieutenant Tudor explained the matter to his interpreter, who then pulled up his dhoti and waded ashore for a long dialogue with the headman, full of head-wagging, arm waving and extravagant gestures essential to Eastern parley, like two gymnasts who have learned differing exercise routines. When Sharif Khan returned he conducted a much shorter discussion with Lieutenant Tudor which the latter communicated to us.

"Mystery solved, men. It seems the natives went for you in a big way, Honners, because you were the first white man they'd ever seen who was smaller than themselves. What with that and finding you in the middle of the ocean without visible means of support they figured you must be the messenger of their sea god, Shuma—or even his son, because your ginger hair is the same colour as the local seaweed."

"Seaweed!" Honners snorted.

"But what really clinched it in your favour was your curved hooter. They thought it was a fertility symbol, like the horn of the rhinoceros is so regarded in parts of Africa and Asia."

"My aristocratic nose!" Honners exclaimed. "So if they ate me their virility would be increased? The cheeky slobs."

"Get it out of your head about being eaten. These delightful folk wouldn't harm a mosquito. They merely wanted you to stay with them to ensure that the population stopped declining through the inevitable interbreeding. That's why you're married to the Chief's daughter."

"Married to Tiddler's tiddler! Words fail me."

"Now you're entitled to draw service marriage allowance." I pointed out.

"Silence, idiot first-class and bar," Honners fumed. "The marriage, as you are pleased to call it, was never consummated because I was too bloated to stand up."

"Men don't normally stand up on their wedding night. Honners—or do they?" I observed.

Honners regarded me down his nose. "Spare me your coarse service banality Pook. The point is that the tenth

Earl of Cudford refuses to entertain the notion that he will be carried to the marriage bed practically unconscious with food, distended by wind and rendered speechless by coconut-fudge being shovelled into his mouth every time he opens it to protest."

Lieutenant Tudor smiled. "Worry no more, Honners. Sharif Khan tells me that custom decrees tonight as the nuptial hour for you and your bride. You see, it is the Feast of Shuma, the big fertility shebang. Pipe all hands to woo. You could start a new dynasty."

Honners shuddered at the thought. "Ah, but we shan't be here. We'll be speeding back to the purgatory of Piccadilly."

"Wrong again. The Chief has invited us ashore for the night and big eats. We dare not refuse their hospitality for obvious reasons. You'll go with the rest of us—that's an order."

"Wrong again. You can't give me orders because I'm dead. You said so yourself."

"Exactly, Honners. But remember Habeas Corpus— we have the body. Thus, according to Fleet Orders, it is my duty to take you ashore for burial. Four Marines either side of the coffin. But I am not a mean man who'd conceal your rights from you. Fleet Orders do permit you to be buried at sea if you so wish."

"I bet you say that to all the corpses," Honners groaned, shrugging his shoulders hopelessly. "Who drew up Fleet Orders—Judge Jeffreys?"

"Do your duty for England, Honners," I advised.

"Once you're safely bedded down at midnight we'll fire a 21-gun salute on the oerlikon," Lieutenant Gull promised.

"That's about all that will fire tonight," Honners said

wretchedly. "You realize this is the end for me as far as St James's Palace is concerned? The College of Heralds will have to work a coconut rampant into our family crest."

"Stop worrying about the future you'll probably never live to see, and stand-to with your wedding-tackle ready for action," Lieutenant Tudor snapped impatiently. "You should be grateful to get a bit of crumpet at all out here in the middle of nowhere."

Honners raised his eyes skywards. "One thing about the Royals—they certainly know how to prepare the eager bridegroom for the happiest night of his life without all that old-fashioned nonsense like romance, church bells and choirboys."

"Well, at least we've got an organ," Lieutenant Tudor laughed. "Now smarten yourself up and get fell in for mating drill."

SIX

We didn't often feel sorry for Honners, and this was another occasion when we didn't feel sorry for him. He ambled ashore, hands in pockets, and when Lieutenant Tudor officially introduced him to the headman, barking the order to salute, Honners very slowly came to attention with his feet apart, then raised the left hand, fingers parted in such a vague manner that the thumb went into his ear.

"Why don't you just salute with your foot and have done with it?" Lieutenant Tudor snapped.

"Can't reach," Honners observed laconically. "As even you must know, I am unable to salute because of an arm accident sustained with the Cudford Hunt when my horse changed places with me and became the rider."

"I heard this rubbish from Colonel Tank, who also informed me that you are unable to say Sir because of a speech impediment sustained at a hunt ball when Lord Liddale had the good sense to punch you on the jaw for your impudence."

"He punched me on the jaw when, in his cups, he objected to my protecting his wife from him. As a consequence I am only able to say Thaw."

"But you don't even bother to say Thaw, man!"

"Surely nobody in his right mind wants to be addressed as Thaw? Besides, in view of my social position it is ludicrous that I should be expected to call any Tom, Dick and Harry Thaw. You should call me Thaw, as you would but for this artificial expediency thought to be essential by the Whitehall warmongers for the successful prosecution of hostilities. Which is patently clear why we're losing it hands down and feet up."

"You insufferable little snob!" Lieutenant Tudor gasped.

"On the contrary, I'm an insufferable little realist. That's why I am unpopular with the unintelligentsia."

While I marvelled, as ever, how Honners regarded the death struggle of the Great Powers merely as an unpleasant interruption in his social life, Corporal Poster ran up the beach towards us. When he reached Lieutenant Tudor he performed a tiny jump in the air, coming down in the rigid posture of the salute—so violently executed that the islanders backed away in alarm lest a white man was having a fit in a manner new to them.

"Sah! Urgent message from HQ, Sah!" he barked, in the peculiar shouting speech essential to Service efficiency. His left hand shot forward like a chameleon's tongue to hand the officer a yellow signal form at high velocity.

"Relax, man," Honners said. "One day you'll do that once too often and drop dead. Did your mother work in an automatic bottling plant?"

"Silence, Honners," Lieutenant Tudor commanded. "Corporal Poster is a smart Royal Marine, whereas you are merely an upright sea-slug. I have heard Sergeant Canyon refer to you as marching manure."

"I prefer not to discuss the lower anthropoids before supper."

Lieutenant Tudor digested the signal intently, his face serious. Then he scribbled a brief reply, seemingly unaware that Honners' nose was almost touching the pad as he endeavoured to read upside-down.

"What did Colonel Tank say?" Honners inquired as Lieutenant Tudor snatched the pad away. "I only got your reply."

"Thank-you, Corporal Poster," the officer snapped.

"Radio my acknowledgement at once."

Corporal Poster leapt into the air for the salute, then rushed back to the landing-craft. Lieutenant Tudor immediately briefed Lieutenant Gull and Sergeant Vile, who recalled all personnel to the boat. Only Lieutenant Tudor remained long enough to explain our sudden departure to Sharif Khan, who in turn transmitted the details to the headman. Like several other officers in the past, Lieutenant Tudor was unaware that Honners was standing immediately behind him, his rabbit ears erect. Honners had so often taken up position behind Lieutenant Titterton in times of urgent discussion that on one occasion when the officer stepped back a pace he actually fell over Honners. Lieutenant Titterton had forbidden Honners on pain of death to stand anywhere near him or to eavesdrop under any guise, such as creeping up to a group of officers holding a button, then, when eventually detected, inquiring if they had lost one.

Being so short Honners was able to stand almost touching Lieutenant Tudor and remain undiscovered even if that officer turned round. It was clear from the conversation that the headman understood the emergency but was requesting that Honners be permitted to stay. Honners' eyes widened as Lieutenant Tudor replied via the interpreter, "Because our common foe comes by ship it is vital that the ginger-headed one goes forth as Shuma's messenger to protect his ocean realm that the Island of Komaddu shall be secure. Little Bhagwati-Nose will, of course, return to you immediately he has destroyed the enemy."

"Bhagwati-Nose!" Honners exclaimed involuntarily, never able to keep his mouth shut for two minutes together.

Lieutenant Tudor span round angrily. "Get to the boat, fool! Can't you see I'm trying to take you with us without unpleasantness?"

"But I'm entitled to object to peurile names. . . ."

"Beat it, you obnoxious little prig."

"Careful how you address a sea god. . . ."

"Don't make me use force in front of the headman, Honners."

Honners raised his arms in ballet pose, then skipped down the beach singing, "I go, I go—swift as an arrow from Cupid's bow. No tears will flow because I don't have to row. . . ."

"Crazy as a drunken parrot," Lieutenant Tudor remarked. "Don't translate that, Sharif Khan."

Our return to Piccadilly Island was overshadowed by the full-scale emergency code-named Operation Chopsticks. This euphemism covered the news that a huge Japanese task force was sailing westwards across the Indian Ocean, so there was no fatted calf welcome for Honners and me. Lieutenant Titterton and Sergeant Canyon greeted us like long lost Japanese prisoners-of-war, their main concern being the fact that we were no longer on ration strength.

"I come among you as one returned from the grave, so rejoice," Honners informed Sergeant Canyon.

"Roight, that's got the bad news over," Crusher growled. "The good news is that your dereliction o' duty got us a proper bumboat."

"Every cloud has a silver lining, as the poet assures us."

"But we're still one crap-bucket short."

"Yet mortal man must struggle on the best he may without the finer things of life."

"We may have to struggle on without you if Lieutenant

Titterton can second you to midget submarines. They're asking for small men of outstanding courage, which sums you up by half."

"Come, my good fellow, don't try to protect my feelings —I know I am also slightly short of stature besides possessing courage. Nobody is perfect—even Lord Nelson was lacking in inches."

"You must have been stunted because all your strength went to your mouth."

"May I point out how Marine tradition placed some dubious virtue on size, as though being grossly enlarged in the body at the expense of the brain manifested some military advantage. On such a premise, an elephant should win the Derby and the Japs should be losing the war. Ha ha ha ha!"

Honners' falsetto laugh rang round the island, as it so often did when he scored a point from anybody, whether it be me or Colonel Tank, who referred to it as the mating-cry of the peacock. Colonel Tank was in overall command of the islands, and now he was visiting all bases to ensure speedy preparation for combat. He was a remarkable man, embodying all that is best in a leader—discipline, intelligence, personality, but above all that imperviousness to personal danger so typical of his breed. Under the terrifying ambience of close action and aerial bombing I saw him issuing orders and observing the state of battle as coolly as if he had been opening a garden fete in peacetime.

Right now he wanted to see the two men who had returned from an extraordinary adventure. After the customary formalities and questions, Colonel Tank addressed himself to Honners, occasionally snorting as if there was a pea stuck up his nose which would not clear.

"I see Lieutenant Titterton has recommended you for

secondment to midget submarines, Honners," Colonel Tank snorted.

Honners smiled superiorly. "As you will be aware from my medical records I am a martyr to claustrophobia, which rules out even giant submarines."

"I am also aware that you are a martyr to every damned thing in the book when you're wanted for action, man. In my long experience you are the only Marine on record who is fit for nothing. Medically you are virtually paralysed—you cannot so much as salute or say Sir; you cannot remain at sea because of a saline allergy; gunfire affects your sense of smell; you cannot march in a straight line because one leg is shorter than the other; you are incapable of obeying orders because bombing has rendered you deaf; Service rations are such that you burst out like a redcurrant bush all over your body; the tropical humidity makes shaving almost suicidal for you. The only thing you've escaped so far is pregnancy."

"As you so wisely observe, Colonel, I suffer terribly. Surely it is imperative that I be flown home to UK? Especially now I have suspected elephantiasis."

"Britain is not conducting hostilities solely for your health."

"Too true. I haven't been healthy since I was called up. I shall soon be a wrinkled old man of twenty-two—if I live that long. Now I've got elephantiasis my time may be short."

"Splendid! Presumably you have elephantiasis of the tongue?"

Honners pursed his lips. "Far be it from me to be alarmist but it could infect the whole Regiment. This is not elephantiasis graccorum—leprosy—but what used to be known as Barbadoes Leg."

"And is now known as Piccadilly Mouth?"

"In your ignorance you jest, Colonel, but you will remember my words when the entire Unit comes on parade with wheelbarrows."

"Wheelbarrows?"

"It appears that the thread-like pallasitic worm, filallia, has gained access to my foot. This will creep up the leg causing chronic obstruction of the lymphatic vessels. Its main attack will be upon the scrotum, producing a spectacular distension of the testes."

"You mean gigantic balls."

Honners winced. "I do abhor this predilection for coarse language which is prevalent among all ranks in the Services."

"We believe in saying what we mean without dressing it up with verbal diarrhoea. That is why you are known throughout the Corps as Slackarse the Fearless."

"I must protest. My illustrious uncle, Admiral Sir Graham Pilkington-Goldberg, VC, DSO, and sundry bars will be ill-pleased to learn that his favourite nephew has been so addressed by a Colonel of the Regiment. As he remarked to Winston Churchill quite recently during dinner with King George the Sixth, when my name came up. . . ."

"Their dinner came up too? Get on with the matter in hand and stop firing your uncle at me. If you must know, Honners, it was he who recommended you to us for midget subs. Who better to stick limpet-mines to the hulls of the Jap warships and sink the fleet, he said."

Honners smirked. "I can hardly be expected to volunteer while suffering from elephantiasis—for one thing they couldn't squeeze me in. On the island of Komaddu I personally witnessed an unfortunate victim of the disease being compelled to carry his enlargement about in a wheelbarrow. Nice state of affairs if the Units here have to parade with wheelbarrows, eh Colonel?"

Colonel Tank blew down his nose with vehemence. "Let me put you in the picture once and for all, Honners. This war is not being conducted as some kind of surgery for your ills. When the present emergency is over I shall instruct Surgeon Commander Campbell to examine your feet, then traverse the short distance along your body to your head. In other words, a complete medical check-up. And if necessary we'll order Marine Bowland to knock you up a small wooden wheelbarrow to keep you mobile."

"Such delay could be fatal. . . ."

"However, medical inspection may not be needed because in the meantime you could well be killed—by either side. If there are any casualties on the heavy ack-ack four-point sevens, you will immediately fill the breach and fill the breech—how I detest puns."

"But gunfire is. . . ."

"Silence, man! Until that arises you will be in the Mobile Repelling Party. You will rush to any point where the Japs are attempting to land and establish a beach-head. Your task will be to drive them back into the sea. You will mow them down until the enemy is repulsed with heavy losses. If necessary you will bayonet-charge them in order to clear the beach."

"Just me?"

"You could do it alone, Honners. But I shall see you are supported by Pook and other suicide-troops. Your motto will be 'They shall land over my dead body.' "

"Sounds like a pretty accurate description of the result."

"Dismiss."

That night Honners and I crouched behind a bush overlooking Beach F on the south side of the island. Sergeant Canyon had informed us that this was our exposed flank where the enemy might attempt to land, so he had posted us forward as observers. We were not to attack single-handed but to alert the main force on our field-telephone. I gazed across the white beach to the ocean and felt extremely lonely. Honners snored contentedly by my side as part of our agreement to keep watches of one hour duration, except that this was his hour of duty and I had awakened suddenly with the guilty feeling that we had not yet loaded our rifles. My watch told me that for the last forty-five minutes we had both been asleep instead of being the eyes and ears of the main defence force, as Lieutenant Titterton had called us.

Having checked that all was well in our vicinity I began to load my rifle. Stores had issued me with two bandoleers of three-o-three ammunition but when I extracted the first clip I was surprised to find the brass ends were crimped where the nickel slugs should be. They were undoubtedly blanks. I checked the bandoleers thoroughly; every one was a blank cartridge. Using the rifle-butt as a weapon I finally succeeded in rousing Honners, then explained the problem to him. He searched his own bandoleer—not a live shell among them.

"It's murder!" Honners fumed indignantly. "They post us out here to die, without so much as a chance in hell! Inefficiency, that's what is losing us this war. Stores can't even tell the difference between blanks and the real thing. No wonder old Tank was bimbling on about driving the Japs back with bayonets. Check your bayonet in case it's a playsafe rubber one."

"I'd better phone Crusher and let him know there's no fire-power up front."

"Ask him if we're supposed to let off the blanks and frighten the Japs to death."

I cranked the handle of the generator on the field-telephone and it turned so easily that I knew it wasn't doing anything at the other end. It had no bite at all. "Phone's dead, Honners. The line must be out of action."

"Or cut. Honestly, this outfit is so inefficient that we might just as well surrender to the Japs while we're still in one piece."

"You'll have to follow the line back to base and see where the break is, Honners."

Honners made big eyes. "Go through the jungle alone at night? You must be crazy."

"Then I'll have to do it."

"And leave me here on my tod to face the foe? Not on your life. Listen to me, Peter. If the Japs try to land we'll raise the alarm with blanks, then run like hell. If they don't come nobody will be any the wiser and we won't have Crusher on our backs like a bear with piles."

"You mean do sweet Fanny Adams?"

"Exactly. What time is it?"

"Midnight, just gone."

"So you're on watch and I can get my head down for a quick kip."

"But you haven't done a watch yet, Honners."

"I happened to doze off because I'm exhausted, that's why. If this is supposed to be war to the death, at least let's be fresh to face it. I'll relieve you at whatever hundreds of hours it is in Service jargon that means one o'clock in the morning."

"One hundred hours."

"As much as that? No wonder the night seems endless."

Honners was able to drop off as though he was worked by electricity and someone pulled his plug out. On this outpost of a remote island I felt extremely vulnerable, the more so for being cut off by phone and lacking live ammunition. It seemed impossible that nothing stood between the base and the Japanese invaders except myself and a snoring body—both of us unarmed to the teeth and unable to communicate with HQ. Honners made no secret of the fact that he hated war and was resolved to sleep as much of it away as possible—he called it hostilities' hibernation—like a tortoise disposes of the winter. His last remark to me before he fell into his present coma was, "If the worst comes to the worst we'll bombard them with coconuts."

At precisely 12.30 I stiffened like a pointer dog, listening intently. The beach was deserted but there were tiny sounds coming from trees on our left flank. Like creaking stairs in a house, so in the jungle no matter how lightly a man may tread he cannot eliminate the minute crackling of the undergrowth as he passes. Instead of trying to wake Honners I placed a hand over his nose to reduce snoring, while I experienced fear in the shape of cold sweat and that indescribable dryness of the mouth. My first thought was that the Japanese had landed elsewhere and were now creeping round our rear.

Because I was peering to the left it came as a double shock to feel something hard pressing into my spine from the right, causing me to scream so loudly that I heard its echo return to me. The gun muzzle pressed me flat to the ground, then several figures ran forward from the left in silence. One of them shook Honners awake, but when he opened his mouth in protest the figure shoved the muzzle of a revolver into it.

So far all I could see was boots, but when hauled to my feet I perceived that the attackers' faces were blackened below their camouflage helmets. Silently they led Honners and me through the trees until we reached the beach near the eastern end of the island; not far, in fact, from Wapping Old Stairs of odoriferous memory. Here we embarked on a small craft like a naval cutter, rowed by eight men. Their oars were muffled and they pulled with that robot precision of the Boat Race till we sped directly out to sea.

I scanned the horizon for sign of a warship but there was nothing visible. However I was able to discern that our course was not straight. Gradually I noticed that we were executing a huge arc outside Loyota Atoll itself, as if we were taking the long way round to one of the other islands in the group. Nobody spoke, not even Honners, whose enlarged eyeballs I could distinguish just above the revolver in his mouth.

As far as I could determine in the darkness we were making for the northern side of the atoll, and my judgement proved correct because the boat went aground on the north beach of Soho Island, the smallest of the group, being about the size of a football pitch. Here Honners and I were pushed ashore in complete silence, but our captors then left us and departed in the boat as mysteriously as they had come.

Feeling euphoric at still being alive I whispered to Honners, "That's a turn up for the books captured by the Japs, yet set free on Soho."

Honners grimaced. "We've been dumped here for one good reason—we can't get off it to escape. Do you realize we're prisoners-of-war?"

"Hell's bells, who's that over there?" I cried. I could

just distinguish two figures against the white sand. "Run for your life!"

"Run! Run he says! Not much point in running round the sea. just the island—and nothing will get me to run into the sea. Just give ourselves up and save time."

I called out, "We surrender. We're unarmed."

"So are we," came the reply. "Is that Pook?"

"Yes. You're Gabby Bilington—I recognize your voice."

"And Tilty Slant's with me. Have you got Honners?"

"Yes. The Japs captured us and dumped us here just now."

"They caught us over an hour ago."

"Why didn't you fight to the death, Gabby?"

"They wouldn't let me. They crept up behind and stopped me dying for my country."

"That's odd," Honners observed as Gabby and Tilty joined us. "You two erks were supposed to be the forward observation post for G Beach. If you had had the guts to raise the alarm Peter and I wouldn't have been taken by surprise."

Gabby shrugged. "What chance did we have? Besides, we found all our ammo was blanks and the field-telephone didn't ackle."

"Same with us. Devilish cunning, these Nipps. Now what do we do?"

"Hit the deck!" I cried, throwing myself into the sand.

"Look north—there's a boat heading straight for us!"

"Two— no, three!" Honners corrected me.

"Shut up or they'll open fire and kill the lot of us!" Tilty pleaded. I knew he was scared because man's primeval fear noise erupted from his trousers as I tried to bury myself in the sand like a ragworm.

SEVEN

The three boats grounded silently on the beach to disembark a lot of men. Apart from a few muffled curses there was no sound, yet so near were we that I was able to identify one man by his oath and huge shoulders. It had to be Sergeant Canyon. If so, the thin little man in front of him could possibly have been Lieutenant Titterton. Surely all our Section had not been captured by the Japs, then assembled on Soho Island to be shot?

Then a strange thing happened. The men trudged through the sand in our direction until I thought they were going to march right over our bodies. But the leader halted and sat down heavily on the sand, whereupon the others followed suit. Worst of all, one of their number sat on me, square on my buttocks. I pushed my mouth onto my arm to prevent any sound escaping, then concentrated on remaining statue-still.

From the corner of one eye I could see the three boats being pushed seawards by their rowers, who then leapt aboard and departed. Only then did anybody speak. It was the man sitting on me.

"Well, the game's up, chaps," he said wretchedly. "We've been let down left, right and centre by the only men who aren't here to share our fate—Pook, Honners, Ellington and Slant. They should be court-martialled and shot."

"Left us ruddy-well exposed as a nudist's backside, sir." Sergeant Canyon agreed.

"Where are they, that's what I want to know?" Lieutenant Titterton demanded angrily. "Ran off in the face of the enemy, I'll wager, so much for our forward observation posts."

"All except Honners," Sergeant Canyon grunted.

"Unless he run off in his sleep."

"Perhaps they were captured like us," a new voice suggested. It was Corporal Crood.

"Captured!" Lieutenant Titterton sneered. "More like surrendered, the cowards. Probably guided the enemy ashore. Not a shot fired, not so much as a tinkle on the field-telephone."

"Then why aren't the slobs here on Soho with us lot?" Sergeant Canyon asked.

Lieutenant Titterton hurred loudly. "I wouldn't put it past that crew to be still asleep at their posts. Nothing wakes Honners, the useless little pig. The entire invasion force could march over his body and he wouldn't know it. What fool detailed him and his precious pal Pook for such a vital assignment?"

"You did, sir. You said they was expendable."

"With respect, sir," Corporal Crood intervened, "would it be possible that they escaped detection and are at this very moment planning to rescue us in some way?"

Lieutenant Titterton laughed bitterly. "Escaped detection, yes. Planning to rescue us, out of the question. That bunch couldn't rescue a cat up a tree. I based my whole strategy on Remplir's classic Mousetrap Defence, and what happens? Those bungling idiots let me down and the mousetrap itself is captured. I, of course, will be blamed for the failure of others, just as Napoleon was blamed for Waterloo. My reputation as a top combat commander has been RUINED!"

As he spoke he brought his cane down with such force on my shoulders that I shrieked with pain and tossed him up in the air. There was general confusion as the four of us were discovered, until Sergeant Canyon restored order.

Lieutenant Titterton seemed unable to absorb the fact that he had been sitting on a member of his observation team instead of a mound of earth, nor could he believe that all four of us had turned up safely.

"The same old story," he ranted. "Directly the action starts my Section is captured to a man. Nobody killed, nobody wounded, nobody missing. The whole damned Section present and correct."

"We like to be with our officer," Honners explained.

"You, Honners—apparently you got here even before the rest of us. Why didn't you phone in the code word to alert us? Why didn't you put up some kind of opposition so we should know the enemy had landed? What did you do—rush down the beach with torches to guide them?"

"We fought," Honners replied indignantly. "We fought bitterly despite blank ammo and being taken from the rear. We did our best with the bayonet, but what chance when you're outnumbered twenty to one? Fight indeed! It took eight men to pin me down."

Lieutenant Titterton sneered. "Eight men to wake you up, more likely. You'll be telling me next that they had to bring up tanks to subdue you and flush you out."

"Then they shoved a blessed great automatic in my mouth."

"I don't blame them either. Pity they didn't fire it."

"Shall we be sent to a concentration camp in Japan, sir?" I inquired hopefully. "I've always wanted to see the Land of the Rising Sun."

My question seemed to make Lieutenant Titterton even angrier, "Of course not, you stupid man. Operation Chop-sticks ends tomorrow and you'll be sent back to Piccadilly island for disciplinary action and intensive training."

"Under the Japanese, sir?"

"Under me, your Section Officer, man. Colonel Tank now knows that there are weak links in our defence system —four, to be precise—and that the islands are not yet immune to enemy infiltration."

"But we were captured by the Japs, sir, same as yourself. We're all prisoners-of-war."

"No, Pook, that will probably come later. This has been an exercise which Colonel Tank disguised as the real thing in the hope that you and Honners would be on your mettle and not turn in for the night directly it got dark. Only officers were in the picture. That is why you were issued with blank ammunition."

"An exercise! Then who captured us, sir?"

"Unfortunately, through your gross dereliction of duty, my well-laid plans went awry when you were taken by the attacking force led by . . . er . . . by Lieutenant Tudor."

"Lieutenant Tudor! If he captured us, sir, who captured you?"

"Well, with my forward observation posts wiped out . . . you wouldn't understand the technicalities of strategy . . . my main mobile strike force was encircled by the enemy and had no option but to capitulate under pressure from er . . . Lieutenant Tudor."

"But only after a bloody struggle, sir?"

"Watch your language, Pook. The engagement was minimized owing to our forces being taken by surprise under cover of night. There was little or no time for effective military retaliation in the shape of a counter-attack or withdrawal to a prepared secondary line of defence."

"First thing we knew was we were prisoners," Sergeant Canyon admitted.

"Were you yourself personally captured, sir?" I queried.

"Of course I was, man! Do you think for one moment I would desert my troops in their darkest hour?"

"In fact you was captured before any of us, sir," Sergeant Canyon added.

"Which is hardly surprising for an officer in the van of battle."

"But they was all round us, sir. You asked me what had happened and that was the last I saw of you till we were all in the boat."

"When Sergeant Vile and Corporal Poster captured me they said Lieutenant Tudor is the sharpest assault commander in the Regiment, sir," Corporal Crood volunteered. "They said even Lieutenant Gull can't compete with him—and he's pretty hot."

"Indeed," Lieutenant Titterton observed coldly.

"They said Lieutenant Tudor will probably be made up to Captain when Colonel Tank sorts this lot out. They said that him being a hotel detective in London before the war makes this job child's play to him, sir."

"Thank you very much, Corporal."

"They said Lieutenant Tudor could have captured us and taken Piccadilly Island the night before, but he didn't because it would have been against Colonel Tank's rules for the exercise."

"Most interesting, Corporal."

"They said Lieutenant Tudor didn't want to attack Piccadilly because it was too easy. They said he wanted to attack Lieutenant Gull on Bloomsbury Island but Colonel Tank wouldn't let him. Colonel Tank said take Piccadilly first, then have a go at Lieutenant Gull on Bloomsbury. That's what he's doing right now, sir. He'll have his work cut out to best Lieutenant Gull, sir—he knows his stuff."

Lieutenant Titterton bored Corporal Crood with his eyes. "Your precious pals seem to have a great deal to say about this unfortunate operation, Corporal, but just let me tell you this, strictly off the record. Once Colonel Tank has analysed the present exercise he has promised me the pleasure of attacking Lieutenant Tudor. Then we'll see who's top assault commander on Loyota Atoll."

"Will you still be with us, sir?" I asked.

"Of course I shall, idiot! Don't you think Napoleon ever made a mistake? Why do you think he lost Waterloo?"

"His forward observation posts were overrun, sir?"

"Because nothing. Imagine I am the Duke of Wellington —the Iron Duke—I see the battle is in the balance towards the end of a long day's struggle. At last I show my hand by throwing in my reserve cavalry. Napoleon is staggered. Victory is mine. Now, what vital lesson do you learn from this, Pook?"

"We must get some horses at all costs, sir."

"No, no, no, Pook. Will you never learn? The great art of warfare is surprise."

"What surprises me, sir, is that you're always Napoleon up to Waterloo, then suddenly you're the Duke of Wellington."

"I'll show you who I am—when the time comes," Lieutenant Titterton grated dramatically.

At that moment Sergeant Canyon drew our officer's attention to a boat approaching Soho Island. "I'll go down to the shore and check this one myself," he said.

"Very good, Sergeant. It's probably the relief boat to take us back to Piccadilly Island."

When Sergeant Canyon departed Lieutenant Titterton

gimletted his eyes and bored them into me. "Listen callefully, Pook, and the rest of you. When our turn comes to attack Lieutenant Tudor on Kensington Island we'll see who is master tactician. He believes his island to be impregnable, but I have found his Achilles heel. Tell me, Pook, what is the most important element of a successful attack?"

"Not to talk about it beforehand, sir?"

"Secrecy is indeed vital, but Remplir says the most important element of a successful attack is to strike where the enemy think no attack is possible. For example, General Wolfe when he stormed the Heights of Quebec. I—and I say I in all humility—have discovered that precise spot. Then I shall lead you to victory."

"We could do with one, sir."

"So much for your Lieutenant Tudor," our officer declared, as though he had already been defeated. "Now as to your Lieutenant Gull, I tell you now that Lieutenant Tudor will never get the better of an officer of his calibre. You will recall how, during your training in UK when we were on Exercise Sea Breeze, I outmanoeuvred the man completely. I encircled his troops, cut off his supplies, drove a wedge between his infantry and the coast, captured his landing-craft and destroyed his ammunition dump. When his surrender seemed inevitable, what happened?"

"We were wiped out, sir. The whole Section was blown up in his minefield."

"So will you be so kind as to tell me why?"

"Because we were attacking his positions which weren't there, sir. Lieutenant Gull was actually following up our rear."

"Exactly. And how did you make such a disastrous miscalculation, may I inquire?"

"Well, sir, Honners got the time wrong. He thought 22.00 hours meant 2.20 in the afternoon instead of ten o'clock at night, and you got the map reference wrong. We were on page 17, whereas we should have been on page 18. We attacked page 17 in broad daylight, instead of page 18 under cover of darkness. So we were completely annihilated, sir. Colonel Tank said it was the first time in his experience that an entire strike force had been wiped out to a man."

Lieutenant Titterton laughed mirthlessly. "You see, one inexcusable lapse by Honners enabled your Lieutenant Gull to slip through my net. So much for his reputation as an assault commander. But mark my words, his luck—and Lieutenant Tudor's—cannot carry them through indefinitely. Skill and true generalship will be rewarded in the final analysis, when I decide to unleash the dogs of war."

Sergeant Canyon came lumbering up the beach and saluted cheerfully, as he always did when bearing bad news. "Lieutenant Gull has arrived, sir."

"Excellent. Has he come to transport us back to Piccadilly?"

"No, sir. He's been captured by Lieutenant Tudor, sir. His Section is arriving any minute."

Lieutenant Titterton bowed his head with tight lips, but did not answer. Sergeant Canyon continued with a fresh buzz. "Lieutenant Tudor is in trouble, sir. Serious trouble."

"He is!" Lieutenant Titterton snapped, raising his eyes hopefully. "Don't tell me the fellow is wounded—badly."

"No, sir. Sergeant Vile tells me he's gone too far, sir, and kidnapped Colonel Tank. The Colonel is furious, saying he is a battle referee, not a combatant, therefore a non-target. Lieutenant Tudor said that won't do in modern warfare, because today small Commando raids are launched specially to capture military commanders, like Montgomery and Rommel up the Desert."

"The conceited bounder should be dismissed the Service for even contemplating such an action."

"Sergeant Vile says they had a proper dingdong, Colonel Tank putting Lieutenant Tudor under open arrest, and Lieutenant Tudor saying that was impossible because Colonel Tank was his prisoner."

"So the blighter is to be court-martialled at last?"

"No, sir. Lieutenant Tudor insisted that Colonel Tank look up the latest Fleet Orders and Admiralty Instructions and there it was, sir. Following recent Commando raids in Africa and Europe specifically to kill or kidnap top brass, all Field Commanders are to take full precautions for the safety of themselves and their staff at all tiimes. That's what done it, sir—*at all times*. Lieutenant Tudor claimed that included exercises, and Colonel Tank couldn't gainsay him, sir. Then Lieutenant Tudor explained how he done it just to show the Colonel how the Japs could have done the same —and Colonel Tank complimented him, sir. Got out the old whisky bottle and started hinting about an early Captaincy, sir."

"Enough, Sergeant," Lieutenant Titterton gulped, as though he had had enough and more. "Let us hear no more of gossip from the rank-and-file. Probably a pack of lies, or gross exaggeration at best. My command is based on facts, and facts alone."

Sergeant Canyon looked nettled. "Well, sir, the facts is that Lieutenant Tudor has captured you, Lieutenant Gull, Colonel Tank and every other stiff on this 'ere Atoll."

Following Operation Chopsticks Lieutenant Titterton became obsessed with the defeat of Lieutenant Tudor, which led to an extraordinary chain of events. Every man was to rise at 05.00 hours and engage in a five-mile run, then do Physical Training until breakfast. All duties had to be carried out at the double—with the result that Honners ran into the Officers Mess tent with the tomato soup and turned Lieutenant Titterton red all over. There were three parades a day, intensive training all day long, night inspections, and what Lieutenant Titterton called Disciplinary Morale Building.

Consequently Honners could not report sick fast enough, this time for a thorough medical check by Surgeon Commander Campbell, as Colonel Tank had promised. Starting at the feet for elephantiasis, the MO worked his way along Honners' body with a fine-tooth comb—and it was the tooth-comb that located the trouble. Honners had head-lice.

"Me!" Honners gasped incredulously. "Pediculus capitas—me!"

"Don't worry, Honners," the MO advised him. "Extremely common in these parts. Almost unavoidable really. All we have to do is to shave your head and treat it."

How we jeered at Honners when he appeared among us like a white egg. The contrast between his sunburned face and virgin skull was remarkable, so that at night it seemed to glow like an upright torch. We advised him to carry a bell and cry "Unclean, unclean!" as he moved about the island, but our derision changed to dismay when the order came for all personnel to have their heads shaven.

We had been brought up on a diet of Hollywood movies set on tropical paradises in the blue ocean, those clinically pure haunts of hula-girls, comical natives and handsome white beachcombers, where the only danger was too much liquor consumed to the plaintive chords of Hawaiian guitars. How different it was in reality. The films had not shown us the mosquitoes and the multitude of flies, nor had those glamorous stars been plagued by intermittent dysentery, prickly heat, dhobi rash—or the dread scrub-typhus. There was no mention of malaria, sand-fly fever or dengue. Nor were the fun and games on the golden beaches marred by all the inoculations and vaccinations we suffered at regular intervals, which in themselves often caused us to feel far from fit.

We seemed to have become a new race of white-domed men who shrieked with laughter at each other until the novelty wore off. Head inspections became a daily feature of our routine to eradicate lice, and it achieved its purpose very quickly. Now our topees were too big for us, wobbling on our heads until we had learned to pad them with cardboard. But something much more serious was to follow, and again this was something we had never heard about, much less seen it on the silver screen of Hollywood.

It all began with football. One of the few recreations open to us was kicking a ball around, and because of the limited spaces on a small island we found the best place to play was on the beaches. There the white sand was not true sand but finely-powdered coral, and we soon discovered that this tended to cut the skin if we fell heavily. Every footballer accepts minor cuts as part of the game but here on Piccadilly it was different. The cuts would not heal. What with the humid climate and our thinned blood, the normal healing process did not take effect. Instead, the moist wounds festered and too often began to ulcerate.

I sustained a cut on the right knee during a tackle, and shortly afterwards it ulcerated, and, worse still, started a chain of small ulcers down the lower leg and on to the foot. Nobody seemed to know what the real cause was or if the coral was poisonous. Some blamed the flies, others said it must be the humidity or the tinned food. Honners made no bones about it by declaring that under the unnatural conditions of the environment our bodies were rotting, therefore we should be flown home immediately.

The MO, Surgeon Commander Campbell, issued me with M & B tablets, like large aspirins, which I had to crush to powder and use as a dressing on the ulcers, nine in all. This treatment slowly improved my condition until eventually I was cured, but others were not so fortunate. It seemed that men who were particularly debilitated by climate and rough living suffered most, because not only did their wounds fail to respond to treatment but grew bigger by the day. For example, Honners had an oval-shaped ulcer on his thigh all of three inches long, and, characteristically, he ordered our chippy, Marine Bowland, to fashion him a wooden leg in readiness for the operation which would follow the onset of gangrene.

Honners insisted on displaying his ulcer to everyone from Colonel Tank downwards, always with the comment, "There's a Blighty wound if ever you saw one! Big as a Christmas pudding."

Colonel Tank wisely issued the order to minimize cuts that there must be no more football on the beach or anywhere else and nobody would be allowed to shave. Furthermore, we were to wear leather gloves when performing any work involving tools.

So now we grew beards beneath our bald skulls, and nicknamed ourselves the Upside-down Brigade. On parade we looked like creatures from another planet, and Sergeant

Canyon delighted to bawl out Honners with, "Face your front, that man! Don't turn round and terrify the rear rank!"

For me this was my very first beard. Some of my friends brushed and preened theirs to bushes of burnished gold, but mine developed unattractively as though I had slipped at breakfast and had an accident with the Shredded Wheat. On one occasion Honners grabbed it under the impression it was some oily-waste we used for cleaning our rifles.

But those with large ulcers were growing worse, till our tented hospital could do little for them. After consulting Surgeon Commander Campbell—and Honners, who limped in to demand a bath-chair—Colonel Tank had no option but to break radio-silence and request the immediate despatch of a hospital-ship to our Atoll. The idea was for our worst cases to be taken on board so that the ulcerations could be removed completely under local anaesthetic.

Directly the buzz reached us that the hospital-ship *Panacea* was sailing from Colombo the magic word Nurses was on everybody's lips. That is to say, all except mine because women have never bothered me unduly and if war decreed that we must spend long periods without female company then I accepted the fact with my customary stoic attitude to life. In any case, women spell trouble—and goodness knows I've had my share of that through trying to help them. My sole concession to the news was that I experimented with cold tea in an effort to tone down my white skull.

Shortly before, we had all heard the rumour that Japanese troops were issued with a rubber woman as part of their equipment, which they inflated to life-size when nature called too strongly. I communicated my views on this subject most vehemently to Lieutenant Titterton on several occasions to assure him that if the Allies adopted such a policy I refused to be palmed off with a rubber woman as a wartime expediency. I pointed out that the next step would be evening dances throughout the combat zones, where the officers would partner the few girls available while the men danced with their inflatable women. I envisaged the possibility of Excuse-Me Foxtrots, with men vying with one another to dance with the most inflated models, and jealous rivals puncturing them from behind. Eventually Lieutenant Titterton forbade me mentioning the topic to him under any circumstances.

When the *Panacea* anchored in the lagoon of Loyota Atoll I was one of the few men who took it coolly. I despised these male weaklings who spent their leisure time peering through binoculars and telescopes for the sole purpose of trying to spot a female of the species, as if they were long-range voyeurs. My concern was to help Honners to get well again and to this end I had volunteered for stretcher-bearer and promised to visit him in hospital every morning, afternoon and evening if hours permitted. Additionally, I had given in my name for the job of courier to show the nurses round the island on a shore excursion, and put in a request to act as liaison link between Piccadilly and the Panacea. Being a stickler for hospitality I had also offered to take our Section Concert Party to the *Panacea* for unlimited shows to entertain the staff and patients, suggesting a matinee, two evening performances and a late night show daily.

I could not see what more I might do to assist Honners, and if I thought of myself at all it was merely to take advantage of the hospital-ship's presence by applying to the Dental Officer to have my teeth checked and scraped.

The effect of the *Panacea*'s arrival was disastrous on my weaker comrades. They talked of nothing else but nurses, and Lieutenant Titterton's intensive training schedule went to pot. Some unscrupulous Marines were not above putting in requests for spectacles, dentures and trusses. Tilty Slant was suspected of trying to catch an ulcer from Honners, and Gabby Ellington made no bones of the fact that he intended shooting off his small toe with his rifle whilst cleaning it. Perhaps Dennis Long most exemplified what men will stoop to when women are scarce, for he returned to camp with his body blazing with the worst rashes I had ever witnessed. It was as though he had bathed in some kind of phosphorescent raspberry jam, but he told me in confidence that he had secretly whipped himself all over with the local stinging nettles.

In order to smarten myself up to visit Honners in his hour of need I washed and starched my best tiddly-do's—khaki shirt and shorts—boned my boots and ironed my puttees. Then I carefully laid the uniform under my mattress for knife-edge creases. Finally, I polished my cranium with strong cold tea to which I had daringly added an Oxo cube.

The fuss the officers made about the nurses was ludicrous. Lieutenant Titterton seemed to regard them as goddesses who were not to be seen, let alone touched or spoken to. No other Ranks were to approach the *Panacea* unless they had been certified by the MO as urgent cases awaiting hospital treatment, and even then they were to be ferried out to the ship under armed guard. I immediately volunteered as an armed guard but it appeared that only NCO's could be trusted with such a vital role. When this childish decision reached me I laughed outright—laughed until I cried. To show my indifference I smacked a chit into the Orderly Room requesting to see Lieutenant Titterton. At the interview I was at pains to impress on him how I had no wish to visit the *Panacea*, to which he replied good, because I wasn't going anyway.

"But, sir, as much as I am loath to leave my post here even for an hour, I feel duty bound to visit my sick comrade —the friend of my childhood, whose parents I solemnly promised I would look after him through thick and thin."

Lieutenant Titterton smiled his bland smile. "That kind thought is no longer necessary, Pook. Honners is fully recovered and ready to report back for duty. I am informed by the Medical Officer that he is so reluctant to leave the hospital-ship that he may have to be discharged by being thrown over the side."

"Our place is here on the island, sir, and to this end I have been elected by the Section as chairman of our Entertainments Committee. The members insist that my first task is to arrange a Welcome Dance for the staff and crew of the *Panacea* as a small token of our gratitude for what they have done for us."

"A dance!" Lieutenant Titterton gasped, as if I had suggested a mass orgy.

"A dance, sir, of treasured memory. Men and women skipping round in time with music, sir—remember? In the past I have organized them wherever we've been stationed, except up the Desert in North Africa when the NAAFI hut was blown up just before we opened."

"A dance on Piccadilly Island! You must be mad, man, Have you in mind a kind of tribal dance for rain on the grass?"

"No, sir. In the mess-tent."

"In the mess-tent! Asking ladies to dance on duck-boards? You'll invite them to come skiing next."

"They won't have to dance on duck-boards, sir."

"Knowing you, Pook, I hope you don't have in mind that they dance on the tables. There's nowhere else."

"There is, sir. When I was in India—Bombay to be precise—we held all-night sessions for a thousand guests in the open air."

"Surely you didn't organize a prayer meeting?"

"The floor was a large area of canvas, stretched tight as a drum by ropes right round the edges. Then throw on bags of French chalk and you're away. Pipe all hands for strict tempo Victor Silvester. Now, sir, that canvas was laid over grass—and canvas is one thing we're not short of. There's plenty of French chalk in the sick-bay and we have our own musicians."

At last Lieutenant Titterton seemed interested. I was on it in a flash. "If you submit your idea to Colonel Tank, sir, it would do our Section good and be one in the eye for Lieutenant Tudor," I smiled, planting the seed.

"I don't approve of that kind of vindictive talk, Pook, so let's have no more of it," he smiled back accidentally. "Do you think you can do it? I mean about the stretched canvas to make a dance-floor. Nobody has been able to overcome the problem up till now, yet you of all people may have come up with the solution."

"I did it in Bombay, sir. I got the idea from the Indians themselves. The secret is the guy-rope through a brass eyelet every two feet right round the perimeter. This makes an ideal floor second only to the real thing. It's the Royals' answer to wood."

Lieutenant Titterton rose from his desk, smacking fist into hand and staring at the picture of General

Montgomery hanging from the tent wall. "By gad, Pook, I believe you've hit the nail on the head at last. Only the other night in the mess Colonel Tank remarked what a pity it was to have lovely ladies amongst us, yet no facilities to hold a ball."

"So get your idea into him while it's hot, sir. Please don't mention my name, sir—after all we did work it out between us, and if you hadn't spotted its value at once it would have been useless."

Lieutenant Titterton preened his small moustache. "Point taken, Pook. I shall throw my whole weight and influence into the affair, so you may rest assured that the Colonel will jump at my idea. What a boost for our Section, eh! Who's top dog now? Dismiss."

Having saluted, I emerged from the tent trembling calmly. Then my legs performed a very strange feat of their own volition by sending me up in the air in a gigantic somersault, like a happy frog. Never before had I experienced such joy at being able to assist my Section Officer in his arduous duties.

EIGHT

Five months without women meant nothing to an iron man like me. I had been without them for longer than that when I was a child, and to me they were merely so many dancing partners. Under the skilled hands—and feet—of my Unde Dick, ballroom champion and top London gigolo, I had already gained my Bronze and only the advent of war had delayed my Silver. I was not known as the Cudford Spectre for nothing, and the Echo referred to me as that master of the creeping hoof.

But enough of my success story for now there was work to be done. First I arranged with Corporal Evans, our sailmaker, to construct the canvas floor. He told me I wanted a drugget, and his professional hands fabricated a beauty. The edges and seams were turned over and butted to make a smooth surface and he sewed in brass eyelets right round the border to accommodate the stretcher ropes. The latter were reefed to tent-pegs for tension, giving us a dancing area of forty feet by thirty feet.

Immediately Colonel Tank gave his blessing to the Piccadilly Ball and Lieutenant Titterton had anounced the following Friday as the date I drew three pounds of French chalk from stores, then assembled the band. This was comparatively simple because we already had the talent, ably led by Marine Ackland on trumpet. There was Tilty Slant on drums and vocalist, Gabby Ellington on guitar, Dennis Long on his mournful clarinet, Corporal Crood on sax and Honners on piano. Unfortunately we did not possess a piano so Honners agreed to run the bar with Sergeant Canyon provided he could solo during the evening by singing his piercing tenor version of *Who From Yonder*

Mountain Calls? This was better really because he could stock the bar fuller than anybody else and I would let him solo at the end of the bar when we wanted our guests to leave.

Our lead vocalist was Gabby, whose imitation of Bing Crosby was quite uncanny, but at the drop of a hat we could muster a barber's shop quartet which brought tears to your eyes if you'd had enough booze.

The bombshell came Friday morning when Daily Orders were posted. Under the heading of Piccadilly Ball Lieutenant Titterton had inserted the dread words, Officers Only.

At once I saw Lieutenant Titterton, who regarded me with the small smirk. "Purely on grounds of numbers, Pook," he informed me airily. "As you well know the messtent's capacity is restricted, therefore Other Ranks cannot be accommodated. As it is there will be a squeeze with just officers and ladies."

"But that means you will have only four ladies, sir. The rest are Other Ranks—plain nurses."

Lieutenant Titterton pursed his lips as if about to whistle, and threw his eyes skywards as though I had uttered a heresy. "Come, come, Pook," he tutted. "Under these exceptional circumstances we cannot exclude some of the ladies. It just so happens that there is not room for all the men."

"But I thought this dance was for the men. . . ."

"I want to hear no more, Pook. In any case it is not good for naval discipline that officers and Other Ranks should mix socially."

"Unless the Other Ranks are female, sir. . . ."

"No insubordination, Pook. Dismiss."

There was consternation on the island when the news spread. Weaker men threatened suicide or defying the sharks by swimming naked to the *Panacea* to take a woman at knifepoint. Dennis Long declared that he would be satisfied just to see a girl. He suggested that a nurse could be brought in a launch to some fifty yards off the beach and wave to us while we jumped up and down and screamed with ecstasy at her. Those who lost all control at the spectacle and tried to swim out to the launch could easily be gunned down in the water. Even Honners had a new lease of popularity merely because he had been on board the *Panacea* and spoken to women.

That Friday morning I secured interviews with Lieutenant Titterton three times, the first to volunteer for the job of MC only to find Lieutenant Gull was doing it. The second, to point out that I would be essential to keep the drugget tight and well chalked. Correct, except that Sergeant Vile was floor-manager. The third interview was a desperate attempt to induce Lieutenant Titterton to put me on as a cabaret act in the shape of an exhibition dance. He said he would love it but unfortunately none of the ladies was up to my standard, and I certainly wasn't going on the floor with Honners as a partner.

At the end of this third interview Lieutenant Titterton went deadly serious, sitting very straight at his desk and barking at me in the dipped accents of military converse. "I will be perfectly blunt with you, Marine Pook, to save further discourse. You—and I mean you, singular—are not coming to the Piccadilly Ball under any pretext. The occasion is Officers Only, your chances of gaining a commission by tonight are slim, you will not bother me for further interviews even if you change sex during the day. In short you are persona non grata for the next twenty-four hours. Dismiss."

That evening the nurses were shepherded ashore

surrounded by a guard of officers as though a Sultan's harem was being moved to a new palace. A ring of NCO's provided a second line of defence, so we stretched our necks as best we could to catch a glimpse of these rare goddesses who were in such demand. Even to hear their voices was bliss. Marine Bates cried out almost hysterically, "I can hear them! I can hear them! They actually sound different."

Ginger Reece's nose was high in the air. "Perfume!" he wailed. "I'll go mad! Oh, what have they done to me?"

Dennis Long appeared to be sobbing with emotion. "It would have been better if they hadn't come," he cried. "I can't stand it any longer. Why have they been sent to torture me like this?"

I stood grimly by, sorry for these weak creatures who lacked my iron discipline and collapsed at the sight of a skirt. As for the officers I despised them for a bunch of sycophants, falling over themselves to curry favour with the opposite sex, fawning and flattering like courtiers of old. Lieutenant Titterton himself was managing to walk with his body half bent, half twisted, that he might smile obsequiously into the eyes of the nurse he was escorting and laugh uproariously at her small-talk. The humiliating spectacle sickened me, so that I was thankful to be not as other men but a rock girt by emotional steel. I turned away in disgust, ashamed of my own sex, and returned thoughtfully to my tent.

The ladies were wined and dined at seven in order that the ball might commence at eight sharp. As the guests arrived at the canvas ballroom the band began to play in that somewhat tinny fashion with a very strong drummy background. The officers milled around the girls in the hope of securing a partner for the first dance, caring little what the band was playing provided it gave sufficient excuse for holding a woman for a few precious minutes.

As yet the band was slightly uncoordinated because, although Marine Ackland was leading it on trumpet, Tilty Slant was also leading it on drums—with a definite volume advantage. I took my time from Tilty because he appeared to be winning just now, rattling the spoons rhythmically on both knees, then running them up my arms with professional ease. At the change of key I used two pairs of spoons, clacking them with the speed of maracas, even double-timing them on my bald bead, then triple-timing them down on my kneecaps.

Dennis was blowing the clarinet almost absent-mindedly while his huge upturned eyes eagerly took in the girls, as if he was piping a snake from a basket and was hypnotized by it. Gabby was strumming the guitar faster than a banjo, simultaneously moaning his heart out on a Crosby lyric, while Marine Ackland was blowing himself red-faced in an effort to take command over Tilty. Like many amateur combinations we were trying too hard at the start, like runners sprinting at the gun with a marathon ahead of them.

Lieutenant Titterton did not spot me until the first waltz because before then he had been fighting a rearguard action to obtain a partner for the opening quickstep, followed by a slow foxtrot. So he hadn't had a chance to survey the band. But now he had won Staff Sister Ingram for the waltz he was handicapped by two problems. Firstly he was so excited by his triumph that he was holding Sister Ingram with reversed arms as though he was the female partner and she leading. Secondly he had forgotten the beat of a waltz to the extent that he had reduced the requisite steps to two instead of the normal three, and was struggling to compensate for the missing step by taking one short stride followed by one gigantic stride six feet long to make up the deficiency. Sister Ingram was unable to stretch her legs six feet, with the result that Lieutenant Titterton suddenly became extremely short as the French chalk took its toll and he performed the splits.

Lieutenant Titterton shrieked with pain as he went down, which was echoed by Sister Ingram's scream of fear as he pulled her on top of him. Many hands assisted their rising from the floor and dusted them off, while Colonel Tank remarked that the place was more like an ice-rink than a ballroom. Lieutenant Gull observed that the impact of his brother officer on the canvas had created a localized fog-bank of chalk dust, causing the onlookers to cough all round the area.

Lieutenant Titterton now abandoned waltz tempo for the safer short shuffle, like a very old man struggling to reach his pub. When he saw me on the band dais his feet flew sideways in astonishment and his head blushed angrily. Lieutenant Titterton always blushed when embarrassed or enraged but since we had been shaven I noticed how his dome went red too. This phenomenon drew my attention to him, for of all the white skulls on the floor his was the only coloured one.

His small new beard twitched agitatedly as he came near.

"So I see you have wangled yourself in as one of the band, Pook?" he chuckled, to let Sister Ingram see how popular he was with his men.

"No, sir—urgent request from Marine Ackland to augment the timpani section. Like this, sir." Expertly I cracked the spoons up and down my thighs, then both arms, then on my bald crown, leering all the while at Sister Ingram.

"Spoons! Spoons in a dance band! Spoons in a waltz of all things!" Lieutenant Titterton leered.

"I think it's absolutely fascinating," Sister Ingram exclaimed. "Really, I've never seen it done before and it's marvellous. How on earth does he do it?"

"One of the little surprises I kept up my sleeve for your enjoyment, my dear," Lieutenant Titterton laughed roguishly. "I give the lead and set the pace, then my men back me to the hilt. Isn't that so, Peter?"

I was so taken aback upon hearing him call me Peter that I giggled inanely and redoubled my efforts on the spoons. A small crowd had gathered round the dais to watch, mainly because the slippery floor had taken the gilt off dancing. At first the victims had laughed sportingly at such fun but now several of our guests were bruised and not laughing sportingly, one lady going so far as to pronounce the drugget a bloody menace unless one wore snow-skis.

Lieutenant Titterton giggled into Sister Ingram's eyes. "So glad you like my little treat for you—Barbara. No lack of talent here in my Section, you see. Peter is just one of my best men whom I encourage to keep up the morale on the island. I don't want you to think for one moment that I am a top combat commander and nothing else. Even though I must be ruthless in battle I never neglect the welfare of my troops. You will find beneath my tough exterior the warm heart of a normal officer, ha, ha, ha, ha!"

I smiled modestly, staring at Sister Ingram as though her hair had caught fire. "My act is nothing really. Anybody can do it. All you need is two spoons, lots of practice and a fantastic sense of timing. I tap-dance too, you know—hence the staccato rhythm. Observe my educated feet."

I jumped to the slippery canvas and performed a fast

time-step plus eleven variations and six sensational wings for a finale, with a flurry of feet that raised the chalk like marsh-gas. The audience broke into a spontaneous burst of coughing.

"I dance so well because I'm a Bronze," I told Sister Ingram. "My Uncle Dick, the celebrated London gigolo, taught me. Back home they call me the Cudford Spectre, master of the creeping hoof. I have danced my way half across the world."

"Didn't that make you extremely tired, Peter?" she inquired, looking at my feet in astonishment.

"Watch me bomb the deck—they call it the yo-yo." I went down for three full splits, up and down like a yo-yo, apparently pulling myself up by my trousers each time I hit the floor. "Follow that, Buster!" I shouted, carried away by nostalgia.

"Splendid, splendid," Lieutenant Titterton said, joining in the applause with a silent mini-clap. "Now let us get on with the dancing, everybody."

Sister Ingram squeezed his arm. "I should so like Peter to visit the *Panacea* and entertain the patients with his act, Roger."

Lieutenant Titterton smiled delightedly with his teeth. "Why, of course, Barbara. I will arrange it first thing tomorrow morning. Now shall we dance?"

"I wonder if it would be possible to watch Peter dancing right now, Roger?"

"But you've just seen him, dear. Wasn't that enough?"

"I mean ballroom dancing. A sort of exhibition. I do love it so."

Lieutenant Titterton forgot to smile delightedly. "Do you want him to dance on his own, Barbara? I doubt if there is any lady here up to Bronze standard."

"Oh but there is. Nurse Birkett was a professional dancer before the war claimed her."

"Is she dead then?"

"No, Roger, she's here. That girl in the green dress dancing with Colonel Tank. Come over and I'll introduce you. You too, Peter."

"Colonel Tank!" Lieutenant Titterton gasped, as if Zeus had descended from Mount Olympus and joined the Marines. "I think Peter had better stay with the band. . . ."

But I was already on my way, laughing archly into Sister Ingram's eyes as I slow-foxtrotted over the drugget at her side, then went into a graceful pirouette to show her how I handled the slippery floor. "Ice-dancing too—runner-up at Richmond, first at the Westover, Bournemouth," I laughed deprecatingly.

"All right, Pavlova, smarten up for the Colonel—we've had just about enough of your showing off for tonight," Lieutenant Titterton hissed in my ear. "Colonel Tank—Sah!"

"Sah!" I barked, springing to attention for the armless salute necessary indoors when hatless.

"Sah" Lieutenant Titterton snapped likewise, but he disappeared as his left foot hit the right foot with robot precision and threw him heavily to the floor as his body turned quarter-circle.

"Very slippery, sir," I explained, helping my officer to rise and dusting him off.

Colonel Tank snorted. "More like an ice-rink than a ballroom. Are you hurt, Titterton?"

"No, sir, thank you very much," Lieutenant Titterton gasped. "All part of the fun, sir. Ha, ha, ha, ha!"

"Dangerous, springing to attention like that under the

circumstances. I see the gusset of your trousers is torn."

"That happened earlier on, sir, during the waltz," I explained. "Lieutenant Titterton took an extra long stride and went down in the splits."

Colonel Tank made the rumbling noise he used for laughing. "A glutton for punishment at work and at play, eh, Titters?"

"Ha, ha, ha, ha, sir," Lieutenant Titterton chuckled wretchedly. Sister Ingram took my arm. "Colonel, we've had such fun with Peter, and now Roger says he can give an exhibition dance with Pamela."

Colonel Tank snorted because he had no idea who belonged to these christian names and he thought dancing was a waste of time anyhow, as he considered everything not connected with the martial arts. He called it idiots' capers, and would have preferred to muster all guests and march them round the ballroom in time with *A Life on the Ocean Wave*. When etiquette demanded that he dance with his wife back in England they seemed to do it by numbers, and Mrs Tank had obviously mastered the art of marching backwards at attention.

"Peter, I want you to meet Pamela," Sister Ingram persisted. "Pamela, this is Peter—and he's a Bronze."

"Sounds like a damned statue," Colonel Tank snorted, but I was not listening because no longer was I staring at Sister Ingram's bun-and-specs image. Instead I was staring open-mouthed at Nurse Birkett, struggling to make agreeable greeting noises to this goddess wearing a great deal of body above her low-cut gown.

"Pamela, what were you called before the war?" Sister Ingram asked.

"Indispensable?" I suggested archly.

"Oh, my stage name was Santalina Amore—quite a

change from Nurse Birkett!"

We all laughed and gasped in polite astonishment because she was beautiful, so I threw up my hands in stunned amazement. All except Colonel Tank, who was one of that vast army of people who possess no sense of humour, yet vigourously deny it. Moreover, he disapproved of anyone male or female—not properly dressed in uniform, and he himself went to bed wearing pressed khaki pyjamas with brass buttons.

"You see, I was a professional dancer," Pamela added, in case we thought she had been a Shakespearean actress.

"Can you match Peter's Bronze?"

"Well, I'll try," she replied shyly. "I was lucky enough to pass my Gold."

"Pure gold," I observed wittily lest anybody else said it before me. "Shall we oblige with a quickstep, Pamela?"

"Love to—Peter."

I knew I was in, and when you were in around the bases of the Middle East and Far East it was every man for himself, what with the scarcity of women and the surplus of men. Not any kind of normal surplus, like two to one, but massive odds—such as ten girls in a Burma base for all us Marines, then having to listen to the bands playing and the thunder of boots as another army of Americans marched in, twenty-thousand strong. We used to play a game at some dances called, not can you find a girl to dance with, but can you spot one without binoculars.

Consequently I snaked rapidly back to the band and asked Marine Ackland for the current favourite we knew so well from our worn records, *An Apple for the Teacher*. "Give it all you've got, Akkers," I advised him, "and beat it to death as fast as you like. Watch me liven this joint up. No more shuffle-shuffle-thud from the plodders but all-action poetry from the sweetest feet in the business. Blow your heart out, Buster!"

Marine Ackland grinned. "If you were a violet you wouldn't shrink, mate —you'd burst into a tree."

I returned to take Pamela from the predators, letting her settle in my arms while we picked up the rhythm and got the feel of the floor surface. This took no more than ten steps before I knew I was embracing a Gold, the sort of partner who is so classy that you have to look to make sure she's there. But she was there all right, one hundred and thirty pounds of assorted charms apparently on rubber wheels.

Now I was on my own stamping-ground—as we call the floor in the trade—I was determined to overcome my natural modesty by giving such a performance that even Colonel Tank would understand why I was not a King's Squad Marine—for surely no man can reign supreme in two fields simultaneously. Despite the drugget and tinny band Pamela and I might have been competing at Hammersmith on a sprung maple floor to the music of Victor Silvester himself.

"No more clumping round with Big Boots," I laughed debonairly as we passed Lieutenant Titterton during the Natural Pivot Turn, Cross Swivel and Progressive Chasse."

"You're a perfect dream, Peter," Pamela smiled. "I haven't experienced anything like this since I joined up."

"Nothing, my dear, nothing—after all I'm just a humble Bronze and you're a Gold. Mind you, I should be a Silver really but they called me up to fight at the wrong time. They wouldn't even delay the war for my Silver."

"How mean can you get!"

"I did not reply because Pamela was giving me plenty of Contrary Body Movement where I least expected it, so my brain had to concentrate and send more strength down to my knees. However, I successfully negotiated the Running Right Turn, Forward Lock Step and Fish Tail, plus the daring Telemark we borrowed from Norwegian skiers.

"Lovely, Peter!" she exclaimed admiringly.

"Yes, I suppose I am, dear—but I do ice-skate too, you know. That and ice-dancing just give me that little sensational edge the others haven't got, perhaps. Let's thrill them with some fancy stuff—Chassé Reverse Turn, Running Zigzag and The Drag, then we'll throw in The Corté for good measure. Why be mean to the wallflowers?"

"No-one can accuse you of that, Peter. What colour was your hair before you were shaved?"

"Oh, a kind of nondescript gold with matching curls, dear. Ignore the beard—it must be a mutation. One of my ancestors probably worked in a mattress factory."

"I find your head most attractive, Peter—quite phallic in a manner of speaking."

"Concentrate on the routine."

I said this more to myself than to Pamela because I was sweating like a fountain—and not because I was on Check and Four Quick Run, Double Reverse Spin or Open Impetus Turn. The truth of the matter was that this talented doll with independent-suspension had finally penetrated my steely armour of indifference to the point where I was struggling to avoid what all top hoofers dread—the Feather Finish on Buckled Knees.

I cursed myself for breaking rule number one, letting one's partner interfere with the ice-cold progression of competitive terpsichore. Extreme knee-buckling had last hit me at Earls Court, when Mavis Cooper thought she was dancing in bed standing up, and I had to pretend that too much alcohol had weakened my legs as she assisted me off the floor during the tango. This so upset me that I wrote to the Dancing Mirror suggesting that men should be allowed to dance together in order to eliminate feminine wiles from such a serious profession, citing this case of Mavis Cooper who had deliberately engineered the malfunction of my patellas in a preliminary heat. I pointed out that the Amateur Wrestling Association had foreseen the danger long ago and sensibly permitted men to hold one another in public.

The theory behind big-time competition is that the man acts as a frame for a beautiful picture of the woman, besides grafting himself into the floorboards with leading and supplying the dynamics of the performance. That is why I had been so successful, because I never became emotionally involved with my partners except Mavis Cooper—and perhaps Linda Matthews, the tall blonde who danced so bow-shaped that she would have unfrocked a bishop, and whose performance had been likened to a honeymoon to music.

Fortunately I am always at my best in an emergency, so I changed gear into the Cross Chassé Quick Open Reverse Turn and Heel Pivot, all of which I was able to execute with my knees locked, rather like a boxer taking a breather on the ropes, giving me time to collect my wits and check my legs for further mileage. However, Pamela's perfume and persistent Body Sway were playing havoc with my usually impeccable coordination. Worse still, a growing illusion that I was embracing a nude woman in public so dominated my mind that I was in danger of collapsing flat on my face if I let go.

Pamela seemed to sense my predicament, and, womanlike, she breathed deeply and nuzzled my cheek with her nose, while her left arm gently encircled my neck in the female version of a half-nelson submission hold. Now I was in desperate trouble, prodding my legs out tripod-fashion solely to support my body either side of Pamela. The question was could a mere woman prop up a two-hundred-pound weakling?

I glimpsed a perplexed Lieutenant Titterton staring at me with his mouth open, like a marathon runner who has lost his way, but it was Honners who came to my rescue. Just as I was praying for the band to jump off the endless roundabout of *An Apple for the Teacher*, all eyes turned to the hall where it seemed that the arduous labour of serving drinks in the hot atmosphere of canvas insulation had proved too much for Honners. While handing a scotch to Lieutenant Tudor and a gin-and-tonic to his partner, Nurse Burton, Honners fell across the bar in obvious distress with a cry of, "Stop rocking the boat, you crazy Bootnecks!"

Sergeant Canyon shouted, "You thieving little slob you're drunk as a lord!"

"I am a lord," Honners groaned. "Why aren't you kneeling to me?"

I pulled Pamela to the bar and leaned heavily on it. "My comrade-in-arms has been taken ill," I informed her. "He's the tenth Earl of Cudford and one of his uncles is a Sea Lord. He's here on a secret mission—midget submarines to sink the Japanese Fleet."

Pamela smiled. "Yes, I met him on the *Panacea* and he told me all about it. Said he'd been selected to win the war single-handed, so he was prepared to die that I might be free. Said I could start by being as free as I liked with him. He also hinted that you were on special assignment too, in Naval Intelligence."

"Don't tell me he blabbed. That's Top Secret Classified Information." I drawled with devil-may-care shock.

"He said you weren't really an idiot but you had to appear

stupid as part of your disguise. In conference with Winston Churchill and Major-General Stickit, Honners' uncle at the Admiralty had chosen you, and to fool the Japanese High Command they called you up as a Marine who obviously had no hope of promotion to Lance-Corporal."

I laughed debonairly. "Ever the little chatterbox. Surely he wasn't so indiscreet as to leak my special assignment to you?"

"I'm afraid so, Peter, because he can't seem to resist women. He said you had been planted here on Loyota Atoll in readiness to be picked up by the RAF and dropped on Tokyo disguised as a geisha girl. Your mission is to capture the Emperor."

"Alone!"

"It can only be done alone, Peter. That's why they chose you—you're so brave. It makes me want to cry."

"Me too."

This startling revelation was interrupted by Sergeants Canyon and Vile carrying Honners from our midst and then administering the latest medical technique for heat exhaustion by heaving his body through the door into the darkness.

"Oh, poor Honners!" Pamela exclaimed. "Those awful men have thrown him outside. He may be badly injured."

"If he isn't he soon will be," I observed.

"As a nurse I must go to him, Peter. He needs proper medical attention. Please come—I can't very well go out into the dark on my own. Someone might attack me."

"How do you know I won't?" I smiled roguishly.

"Oh, that's different—darling Peter."

Suddenly for the very first time I found myself taking a new interest in Honners' welfare.

NINE

I smiled esoterically at Pamela to let her know I perceived her natural feminine desire for me and understood. Why, I asked myself, had Nature fashioned me in a mould so attractive to women, yet at the same time had made me almost immune to their wiles? Here were all these officers and men panting for a mere glance from a matron, while I had unwittingly become Mister Right for the most gorgeous girl on the *Panacea*. What was it about my frigid masterful bearing that caused the opposite sex to become my willing slaves?

As I went to follow Pamela through the door my way was barred by Lieutenant Titterton, obviously not in party mood. In fact he seemed extremely tense, as if undergoing a charge of static electricity. "Where do you think you're going, Marine Pook?" he demanded in his parade-ground voice.

"To help Honners, sir. He's suffering from heat stroke."

"Oh no you're not—you're chasing Nurse Birkett."

"She did ask for my assistance, sir."

Lieutenant Titterton's lips were actually trembling. "Listen to me, Pook. You inveigled yourself in here as part of the band, and now you think you're going to molest Nurse Birkett. This social evening is for Officers Only, not for Other Ranks, understand?"

"But Nurse Birkett is an Other Rank, sir."

"Heavens, man, she is a WOMAN!"

"I know, sir. I spotted it immediately we were introduced," I replied puzzledly. "I've danced with hundreds of them in the past. They go backwards while the men go forwards."

"And they have babies too," Lieutenant Titterton sneered. "I realize only too well that you can identify a female better than a rutting moose, but you are not going to take advantage of Nurse Birkett—and that's an order."

"Then I had better tell her at once, sir. Ladies don't like to be kept in the dark—ha, ha, ha, ha, sir!"

I chuckled to let him see it was a witticism but he was in no mood for banter. "I forbid you to go near her, Pook. I personally shall protect her while she tends your drunken little friend—accompanied by Sister Ingram, naturally. You will be better employed taking Honners' place behind the bar under the watchful eye of Sergeant Canyon."

"But she needs me, sir."

"Nurse Birkett needs you like a boil on her pretty nose. Quick march to the bar, Pook."

"But she was captivated by my dancing, sir. She wants me to walk her home."

"Good heavens, man, this isn't your Cudford Palais. You don't act the belle of the ball here, then pick up some little tart and walk her home for all you can get. Nurse Birkett is a guest of the officers!"

"But you were only called up for the war like me, sir. Honners says that in civvy street you were an insurance agent working on commission. We're not real Marines like Colonel Tank is. I was a bank clerk and Honners was studying to be a solicitor."

Lieutenant Titterton's face elongated with shock, as though a giant soldier ant had penetrated his underwear and nipped him in the bud. "Lése-majesté!" he gasped.

"Who's he, sir?"

"Treason! One more remark like that, Pook, and you'll find yourself under close arrest."

With characteristic cunning I sprang to attention for the hatless salute due to Mars, the god of war, simultaneously barking, "SAH!" because if he put me under close arrest my love life would be in the same category as the self-fertilizing worm.

"That's better," Mars replied. "And forget about any wild visits to the *Panacea*, Pook. We'll leave entertaining the patients in the capable hands of ENSA, understand?"

"Sah!"

Determined not to let Pamela down I put my problem to Honners on the morrow. Honners was on open arrest following the drink charge, which meant, according to him, that "I must not leave the island by walking about the Indian Ocean without an escort, or fly up into the air without permission. Nor may I run, in case I suddenly leap off the island and land on Asia. Hence I need only wear my best ball-and-chain for those romantic evenings by candlelight with Crusher."

Honners and I scoured the island for anything in the shape of a boat that could possibly transport me to the *Panacea* by night, but everything floatable had been removed or was under constant guard. The *Panacea* stood some four cables off in the lagoon. I knew this because all the regular-service Marines said so, yet they didn't seem to know how long a cable was. I put the question to Honners.

"My dear fellow," he yawned, "I don't know if you have led an extremely sheltered life in some Alpine monastery but your general knowledge does not appear to embrace the very frontiers of science. How you ever mastered the art of walking upright defeats me. One nautical cable is one hundred fathoms. Now you probably think a fathom is half a hundredweight, but in fact it is six feet or two yards.

Therefore we deduce that four cables are eight hundred yards —nearly half a mile in common parlance."

"So if we can find transport you can direct me to Pamela's cabin."

"No, Peter—if you can find transport I can brief you as to the exact location of her cabin. I'm not coming because Titters has put me down for chains, flogging and hanging from the yard-arm, in that order, if I leave the island by so much as one inch. The uniformed idiot has even forbidden me to paddle for the relief of my sore feet."

"So all I need is a boat."

Honners grinned superiorly. "There are no boats, Peter. But they have overlooked one source of buoyancy. Look over there at the MT Section."

I looked as requested. "I can't drive a Matador truck over the sea, Honners."

"No need. Where there are trucks there are inner-tubes. Watch this, loverboy."

Honners led me over to the MT sheds where a dozen tubes were hanging from racks. "You want two tubes, Peter, one to ride on, one spare in case you collide with a swordfish or something, towed behind on a length of rope."

"Marvellous, Honners! But what about a paddle?"

"Nature has provided hundreds. Observe the butt end of the coconut-palm branch—a perfect slightly triangulated paddle when stripped and cut to size. After all, you're not rowing home to UK."

"Fantastic!"

"Nothing, chum—just my normal genius. You ride clear of the water on a hunky big Matador tube, towing behind your life-boat in the shape of a small tube from a fifteen-hundredweight truck, see?"

"I'll never listen to other people again, Honners—you're not all bad. You've really saved my bacon this time."

"Ignore jealous peasants, Peter—you know pure gold when you see it. I'll be best man at the wedding."

"Now let's get organized for tonight—Operation Gondola!"

"Just promise me one thing, Peter. If something goes wrong, like they nab you or the sharks tear you to pieces, don't mention me. Titters figures I could get thirty years when he finds out where all my hooch and stock come from, and he suspects I've hidden those antiques I picked up in Egypt somewhere on the island. No good telling him it was the old-time pirates buried it here. So I don't want him pinning homicide on me as well."

That Saturday midnight Honners helped me roll the big Matador tube into the sea, then pushed me gently clear of the beach. Twelve feet behind me the small tube floated securely on its rope in case of accidents. I sat fairly comfortably astride the tube, just clear of the water and pleasingly impressed by its stability and size. My chief difficulty was the paddle, which tended to rotate the tube unless I kept changing sides—all with precious little progress towards my goal.

The solution hit me after ten minutes of struggling to stay clear of the beach. All I had to do was to paddle with an upright stroke inside the circumference of the tube. This method of operating the paddle back and forth between my legs was far more efficient, less tiring and easier for me to keep on a straight course. Fortunately the sea was mirror calm, and by glancing over my shoulder from time to time I was able to check that I was progressing surely, though slowly. Even so, I foresaw this could well be the longest half-mile of my life, yet I was determined to make it at all costs.

I kept a wary eye open for sharks, wondering if they slept during the hours of darkness, or, like the dolphins, they snatched their slumber in short dozes of one to five minutes on the surface. I don't recall spotting any sharks, though there were dolphins about. In my lonely position I found this quite a consolation because Honners had told me how dolphins gang up on sharks, form a circle, then rush them at thirty miles an hour to batter them to death with their blunt heads. He told me how five 300-pound dolphins working as a team could defeat any shark, yet dolphins—or porpoises as the Americans call them—were the only creatures who loved man without any strings attached; not so much as cupboard love. In fact, Honners had a Roman coin depicting a boy riding on the back of a dolphin for the sheer fun of it, and he reckoned they had a brain slightly heavier than man's 3.1 pounds weight. I loved dolphins, and tonight I prayed that this would communicate itself to these intelligent mammals so that they would love me back, particularly tonight.

Once in Ceylon, standing high up on Swami Rock above Trincomalee, Honners and I had watched the dolphins sporting far below in the tidal race and he had remarked how they reminded him of me. I felt flattered, being a strong swimmer myself, and having learned how the resilient skin of the dolphin adjusts to the contour of the water with such efficiency that friction drag is reduced by anything up to ninety per cent, enabling them to outrun an ocean liner. However, Honners explained that the resemblance he meant was in the face, especially the wide mouth and small eyes when I smiled.

By now we had learned more about the tides in the lagoon, so that my rubber gondola was on course for the *Panacea* along a gently curving arc. My arms ached and the astride position was not doing anything for my legs, yet at the halfway mark I seemed to find my second wind as the thought of my lovely Pamela loomed ahead. Honners had given me detailed instructions for embarking and locating her cabin. As the *Panacea* swung at anchor I could already distinguish the gangway on the port side, which was kept lowered in position for legitimate business to and from the islands. Honners had advised me how this entry was rarely guarded during the small hours and that I should experience little difficulty in gaining access to the ship without detection. In my pocket was the plan of B deck which IIonners had drawn, containing the vital information concerning the safe route to Pamela's cabin. He had even marked objects like store cupboards and toilets, with the warning: "Hide in here if coast not clear."

Although I could see the *Panacea* very clearly I felt certain that nobody on board would be able to detect the small black dot on the ocean that was an inner-tube containing me. My head throbbed excitedly as the great hull loomed above me and I was no longer paddling towards a vague shape but actually directing my craft to the landing-gangway. In fact I was so close that I could ascertain that nobody was visible, on duty or not. All that remained to do was to secure my bulbous craft to the rear of the landing-stage where it would be out of sight, then ascend the ladder to my beloved.

Then it happened, and I have never revealed this to a soul until now, with the exception of Honners—and he believes me to this day.

Without warning my circular raft took on rapid motion, so rapid that I was forced to cling on for dear life or be thrown into the ocean. I was going through the water like a speedboat, creating quite a bow wave on either side, and frankly I was terrified. Directly I had collected some of my wits I noticed how the tube had changed shape to an extreme oval, due to the fact that it was being hauled along by the towline with frightening force.

When I discerned the source of such power I could not believe my eyes, for there ahead of me was the smaller inner-tube and it was plain to see how it was hooked round the neck of some kind of monster from the deep. Instinct told me to throw myself clear, yet a second instinct was warning me to cling on rather than risk becoming shark-fodder. So, lying flat with both bands grasping my end of the tow-rope I spread my legs wide for better purchase and conducted an instant prayer service for my preservation.

There was no doubt in my mind now that the giant up front pulling me with the urgency of a diesel express was a dolphin. Not your seven-footer of the Atlantic but the tropical ten-footer we had come to recognize in these waters. There was no mistaking the gunmetal hide and the almost human head—and at this range I was able to distinguish the single nostril at the crown, that crescent-shaped blowhole through which he breathes and is also the source of his voice, for he can vibrate it like human lips.

In reflection I don't suppose my nightmare journey could have been much more than a minute's duration, yet to me it seemed hours as I experienced all the symptoms of extreme fear from dehydration of the mouth to incontinence of the bowel. Without warning I found myself in shallow water, scarcely moving—then a huge snout nudged me onto the beach. The creature had actually pushed my body clear of the water, together with the big Matador tube. As I lay there petrified, feeling as Jonah must have felt after his trip by whale, I was astonished to see the dolphin sporting about in the shallows, and, more eerie still, emitting a kind of high-pitched whistling chuckle.

I dragged myself up the beach crocodile-fashion because my legs had ceased to function, and I had to check twice to ensure they had not been lost en route. I feared that if I remained near the water the dolphin would drag me into the sea for more fun and games, so my survival instinct drove me on until I had crawled and rolled right into my tent. I lay on the floor gasping for Honners, who slept as near death as a human can without actually being buried, finally seizing an overhanging leg and pulling him off the bed onto me.

"What uniformed gorilla fell off his tree to wake me up?" Honners demanded angrily. "Even Napoleon needed five hours kip—or is this the new exciting 3 a.m. reveille for early breakfast to lengthen my working day to twenty hours? What does Titterton think I am—a blessed owl or something?"

"It's me—Peter," I gasped.

"Ok, so you've had what other men merely dream of now sleep it off. Tell me the sordid details in the morning. Crash your swede before Ackland goes berserk on his bugle for another day of bliss under Crusher."

"I'm scared, Honners."

"Not half as much as Pamela, I'll bet. Now die quietly."

"But I didn't get there."

"What do you expect on the first night—a white wedding?"

"I mean I didn't make the ship. It was horrible, Honners. Just as I drew level with the gangway I was rushed back to shore by a dolphin."

"Dressed up as her outraged mother, one presumes?"

"I don't expect you to believe me, Honners, yet it happened. That's why I'm lying here a trembling wreck. It was horrible. I could have been killed."

Honners lit a torch, then produced a bottle of scotch from the shadows like a conjuror. "You're obviously in a bad way, Peter, so have a drink—you can pay in the morning—and tell me exactly what happened to ruin your night of love."

Gratefully I sank the liquor and related every detail of my adventure. When I had finished Honners nodded wisely. "I do believe you, Peter, partly because you don't tell a good lie and partly because history is littered with tales of the Delphinus delphis helping man. Even today we read of them actually saving folks from drowning, guiding ships through difficult channels and generally behaving like vigilant coastguards. This one might have spotted your face and thought you were his cousin. Be that as it may, dolphins have this one defect in their character that they like man and will go out of their way to assist him or play with him— which is good enough reason for me not being a dolphin."

"I'm really glad you believe me, Honners—I just had to share it with someone. I thought living on this island might be driving me crazy. Poor Pamela—looks like she's lost me."

Honners smirked superiorly. "Good news, loverboy. The solution to your problem came to me earlier tonight when I was preparing myself for slumber."

"Forget it, pal. I can't swim through sharkville."

"No need. Listen. This is Top Secret, but down in MT is Lieutenant Titterton's pride and joy, covered only by a tarpaulin. A Carbo—sent out here for trials under tropical conditions."

"What the devil is a Carbo, Honners?"

"Well, this is Classified Information, but the Government is working on a kind of Jeep that will be amphibious—half car, half boat, see. *Per Mare, Per Terram*, remember?"

"A floating Jeep!"

"Exactly. Driven by a small propeller astern, guided by the normal deflection of the front wheels. Motor down the beach and straight into the water, then chug-chug swiftly across the sea to the *Panacea*, park without lights and fall into the arms of your honey."

I gazed at Honners with unaccustomed admiration. "You're sheer genius, chum. But if this is so Top Secret how come you know all about it?"

Honners closed his eyes and pursed his lips. "One of my punishment fatigues—number19, I believe—imposed upon me by Titters as a manifestation of his insane jealousy and class hatred, requires me to sweep the island and dust the trees daily, not to mention washing the reef at low tide. So conscientious me always starts on his desk and filing-cabinet in the Orderly Room, tidying his papers as I dust away merrily singing an old English spying ballad. Then I chat with his batman, Tilty, and pass the time of day with Paddy Ryan down in the MT workshop. In this fashion a pattern seems to emerge until I know more than Titters himself. You see, he hopes to use the Carbo in the next big Exercise and spring a surprise on Tudor."

"Does Tudor know?"

Honners smiled mysteriously. "Just you worry about seeing Pamela. I'll fix it with Paddy that the key will be left, in the Carbo, and tomorrow night you can drive down the beach and out to the *Panacea* in a matter of minutes."

"Sounds fantastic, except for one snag, Honners. I don't know how to operate the thing."

"Love laughs at locksmiths," he sniggered. "You can drive a Jeep, can't you? The only difference is that you engage a special gear directly the tub is afloat. It's marked Prop. This activates the propeller instead of the wheels. There's even reverse, all clearly marked for easy control. As for steering, you use the wheel as on land. An idiot could drive it, so you should have no bother."

"But suppose Titters were to catch on what I'd done?"

Honners sighed loudly. "He'd murder you, of course— but you've got such a build-up of lust to work off that if you don't chance it you'll explode. I can't do any more for you unless I capture the bloomin' *Panacea* myself and beach her while you wait on shore armed with a ladder."

"But he's bound to find out, Honners."

"Not so, little friend of the dolphins. You return the Carbo before dawn, park it smartly in the MT shed and who's to know? Paddy will cover for you by washing it down before Titters has finished breakfast. In any case he's too busy on admin and Daily Bumf to check before midday. If Pamela is potty and goes for you in a big way you could drive out to the *Panacea* every night till she sails."

"So I'd really be helping Titters test the Carbo, wouldn't I?"

"Naturally, but I don't advise you to put it to him like that. All I ask is that if anything goes wrong don't drag me into it. At least give the Japs a chance to kill me before Titters does."

"Thanks a million, Honners," I said sincerely. "I never appreciated your friendship properly until tonight. Perhaps soon I'll be able to do the same for you."

Honners swigged the scotch. "Forget it, Peter. Just volunteer to take my place against the war when they shoot me."

Sunday midnight found me creeping to the MT sheds with a sense of high adventure. Shed 3 was unlocked, just as Honners said it would be, so I entered and shone my torch carefully. There were five jeeps lined up facing the long way, then a space, then a vehicle covered by a tarpaulin, exactly where Honners had told me. Removing the cover revealed an open vehicle similar to a Jeep, and, having driven them in many lands, I was able to put my hand straight on the ignition key.

The engine—20 horsepower according to Honners—purred satisfyingly to my touch as I reversed out of the shed and motored carefully down to the beach. This seemed the ultimate in travel, four-wheeled drive on land and now the new conception of water no longer presenting an obstacle. I had heard about the jeeps fitted with schnorkels which enabled them to negotiate shallow rivers but they did not float like this job, merely submerging to drive across on the river bed. Because of my luxurious transport I had donned my best tiddly uniform to impress Pamela, complete with topee to cover my bald head.

Extremely excited by the novelty of the Carbo and the joys that lay ahead I drove steadily into the sea, yet not so fast as to splash my finery. The four-wheel drive responded magnificently, taking me through the water until the level had risen well above the tyres. The beach shelved steeply, so I decided it was time to cut to the propeller drive, but now I was surprised to discover that the gear lever was surrounded by water.

The vehicle continued to go forward down the slope of the beach and now the water-level was just above the front of the bonnet. The engine cut out but the Carbo still ran down the slope without floating, and to tell the truth I could no longer see any of the bodywork. The sole item above sea-level was my head, and I began to wonder if this clever invention worked on the submarine principle. I could still feel the car progressing forward and downward but I could not remain in it because my buoyancy caused me to float out of the driving-seat.

My first instinct was to strike out for the beach, some fifty yards off, but I checked myself when a terrible idea occurred to me. Although the vehicle had disappeard entirely there was still a great deal of bubbling taking place, so I could locate the body with my toes merely by treading water. With a neat somersault in the warm sea I dived down five or six feet to examine the rear end of the chassis. After several dives coupled with a systematic groping search in the darkness I had established beyond doubt that nothing in the nature of a propeller had been fitted to this buggy.

That could mean only one thing—that I had swallowed the tale about an amphibious Jeep and Honners had sent me to disaster yet again.

My best uniform had been ruined, my love life wrecked, and I had lost a service vehicle in the sea under the most unexplainable circumstances. Therefore it was essential I reach land immediately lest I had a fit and drowned in my own depth.

Honners was the most unpopular man in the Regiment for a variety of reasons and at all levels. Lieutenant Titterton hated Honners more than the Japs and was doing his best to have him transferred to midget subs. Sergeant Canyon had previously broken Honners' nose following the chaplain's sermon on Who is My Brother?—and Honners' declaration that "if Crusher is my brother I'm switching to the Moslems first thing Monday morning when their mosque opens." And among the rank-and-file there was a general feeling that Honners should be dropped behind the enemy lines wearing a concrete parachute.

I was currently having extremely unchristian thoughts about my ex-friend, such as sawing his head off with a breadknife while he slept, or giving him a hand-grenade sandwich. In fact, it was remarkable how many people seemed to think that Honners' character would be greatly improved by a violent death, and now they had my full support.

One could not help noticing little things about Honners, the way he never received or sent any cards at Christmas, and once at his birthday party in Cudford his Uncle Clarence had presented him with a writ.

I entered our tent and did something I had not even thought of before. I pressed the point of my naked bayonet into Honners' throat until he woke up, then kept it there to extract a confession.

"I wouldn't pull a mean trick like that on the old buddy-buddy of my childhood!" he whined directly he got the message. "Of course the Carbo is there, Peter—you must have taken the wrong truck."

"I took the one covered with a tarpaulin, mate, like you told me to. Now I'm going to slit your lying little throat and do the whole Regiment a favour."

Honners was obviously alarmed by my wild eyes and bayonet pressure. "I expect Paddy Ryan whipped the cover off and put it on a standard Jeep so as to be all ready for you, Peter. For pity sake take this tin-opener out of my gullet so we can rectify matters. We'll give Paddy a shake, then he can prove I'm telling the truth."

"If you're not, Honners, you'll have to be transferred to the WRENS after I've finished using this bayonet on you."

Paddy confirmed that the Carbo did exist but he could not explain how it came to be uncovered. Worse still, he was alarmed to discover that the vehicle I had lost was Lieutenant Titterton's personal Jeep. This revelation so upset Honners that he was forced to cry into his handkerchief.

"Oh, Peter, of all the trucks here you had to pick on Titters' favourite runabout. It'll break his heart like it has mine."

"I'll deal with you later, you scheming little rat. You're evil. No one else would have sunk so low as to switch the tarpaulin to Titters' personal Jeep."

Honners creased his face in imitation of something he could never accomplish—shed tears. "Me! But I'm a goodie."

"You'd do anything to get even with Titters. You're a rat, first-class, with ball and clasp. Everybody says you're Hitler's secret weapon, and Crusher calls you marching manure, and Puffy says you're an upright toad with boots."

"Sticks and stones may break my bones but names will never . . . ."

"Even the Chaplain says you're mentioned in the Bible under the name of Judas in case you sued the publishers for libel."

"More like the Good Samaritan after all I've done for you and Pamela."

"Stop arguing, both of you," Paddy advised. "Peter can still go ahead in the Carbo, then I'll shake Johnny Trott and between us we'll drive a Matador down the beach and winch out the Jeep before sunrise."

"But the tide is coming in," Honners observed smugly.

"How do you know that?" I snapped suspiciously.

"When you consider that I am mathematically competent to calculate astronomically the precession of the equinoxes, it is surely not beyond the wit of man to comprehend my familiarity with the local tides, Peter."

Paddy smiled at Honners' pomposity. "If Johnny and me can get a block-and-tackle down to the Jeep, the Matador will winch it high and dry to the beach in no time. We've done it with tanks before now."

"You're a real pal, Paddy," I exclaimed, "not like some of the vermin around here who knife you in the back for their own ends."

Honners tried hard to look deeply wounded, but he could not manage it, nor conceal his satisfaction over Lieutenant Titterton's Jeep. Paddy reversed the Carbo out for me, then, with a few basic hints on how to handle it, drove me down to the beach, then saw me safely into the water.

"Don't worry about the Jeep, Peter," he reassured me. "We'll fish it out and tell Titters it's due for maintenance."

"Thanks a million, Paddy."

"Now go off and love her up, you jammy devil."

Almost unable to believe my luck I steered for the *Panacea*, sallying forth to carry out that precept I had learned at my mother's knee —Ladies first.

TEN

Pamela Birkett was the toughest woo I ever tackled. When fellows complain about their love life being difficult I laugh at such banality, wondering how they would fare if their party was a nurse immured on a hospital ship in the tropics, surrounded by an ocean infested with sudden death in the shape of everything from sharks to electric eels. I still believe I gave the best ten years of my life to Pamela compressed into two nights which haunt my dreams to this day. In fact, Paddy Ryan remarked afterwards that if they awarded medals for courage in love beyond the call of duty I would have received the VC and a disability pension from the Daughters of Britain Guild.

The Carbo purred smoothly out to the *Panacea* without incident, enabling me to make fast to the landing gangway at the end hidden by the steps. Creeping silently up to the entry I automatically saluted the quarter-deck though there was not a soul about. Having memorized Honners' route map and instructions I turned right and made my way along B deck in the direction of Pamela's cabin. So far so good.

My luck broke halfway down the deck, for in the distance I heard voices—one male, one female—whom I supposed to be a doctor checking with the night sister. Without a trace of panic I recalled Honners' warning to hide in a toilet located just ahead to my right, marked WC on his plan. My heart warmed to Honners as I found the WC door just as he had said. It was shorter than normal doors but I opened it gratefully and ducked inside.

Then an extraordinary thing happened. The floor gave under my weight, as though it was hinged where it met the wall, so that I had no option but to slide down it like a trap-door. It stopped at an angle of forty-five degrees with a metallic clang, transferring my body very smoothly onto a kind of alleyway that descended steeply. There was no halting myself in the darkness as I experienced the sensation of travelling downwards at high speed.

Suddenly I lost contact with the floor and underwent the horrific feeling of plummeting through space feet first. I hit the sea with such velocity that it seemed minutes before I could regain the surface, yet even under such conditions the thought flashed through my mind that Honners' WC was the naval abbreviation of Waste Chute. As I cleared my mouth of water I asked myself was it possible that within six minutes of leaving the Carbo I was once more floundering in this cursed ocean that had cost me so dear.

But all such thoughts, such as what would be the reaction of Honners' parents when they received his ashes in a glass egg-timer, deserted me as I struggled to reorientate myself. I was some sixty feet aft of the gangway so I threw caution to the wind by swimming for it like a paddle-steamer, churning up the water as a shark deterrent lest the carnivores had heard supper arriving like a meteor from the sky. I was also anxious to discourage man's best maritime friend, the dolphin, from rescuing me by rushing me to the shore on his snout, as though I was an elongated beach-ball.

Hauling myself up onto the landing-stage I retired behind the ladder to wring out my clothes rather than leave a trail right to Pamela's door. Yet how could I be sure it was her door? Would I knock softly at cabin 37, as Honners had specified, and find myself in the burly arms of Surgeon Commander Mountjoy-Holmes, DSO? I experienced that feeling so common to all who knew Honners, a sense of helplessness coupled with a primeval urge to tear him to pieces with my teeth.

On this my second attempt I reached cabin 37 without mishap, to discover the problem resolved because below the number was a small brass cardholder with Nurse Birkett's name thereon. Scared to make a noise by knocking, I tried the handle. The door opened easily, so I slid inside, closed it, then knocked gently on the side of a bunk I could just discern in the gloom.

"Who's that?" came a voice.

"Me—Peter. Your dancing partner on the island. Remember the ball on Piccadilly?"

"Peter!"

One thing about nurses, they're trained not to panic in an emergency. Pamela switched on her bunk reading light and blinked herself awake. "You're soaked!" she gasped.

I chuckled debonairly. "Calling for you isn't easy, honey. Your place is surrounded by water."

"Heavens, don't say you swam out here!"

"I came by launch—small enough to be damp, ha, ha, ha, ha!" I skipped the Waste Chute incident as strictly unromantic.

"But you're practically dripping, Peter. Get those clothes off at once. I'll dry them under the deckhead blower on that line, like I do my own."

Poor girl, she couldn't wait to strip me, I reflected happily. Women are strange creatures because here alone in a wartime hospital ship Pamela was wearing a pale blue nightdress resembling a petticoat that had shrunk in the dhobi. As she hung up my kit on the line I observed her long legs and everything they supported. Such a gorgeous silhouette would have affected weaker men but I merely surveyed her calmly as I knelt down on the floor to rest. I didn't want to rest but somehow my knees had gone to sleep, giving me no option.

Pamela noticed my change of position and said, "If you're shy, Peter, wrap yourself in this." Whereupon she tossed me a face towel as big as a handkerchief. I smiled bravely to let her see how the spirit was willing but the knees were weak.

"Oh you poor boy!" Pamela exclaimed compassionately, parking my face on her bosom as she helped me to rise. "Just you lie on the bunk a while to recover."

"Thank you, nurse. I am pretty well bushed."

"So I should think after all you've been through."

"It's been more than six months since I've even seen a. . . ."

"What with horrid rations deficient in vitamins, awful living conditions on that wretched island, bugs and germs all over the place. . . ."

"And no women," I reminded her in case I ended up with a bottle of iron tonic and a gargle.

"After your ordeal I wonder you've enough strength left to think about women, Peter."

"After six months one can't seem to think about anything else, darling. That's why I risked my life getting here," I growled virilely.

"I am a woman, Peter," she smiled to show me she understood the male-female syndrome, then leaned over my body to show me that she was indeed all woman. I feared I might pass out at the sight of so much surplus evidence, like a starving man who collides with a hot-dog stand.

Pamela slid her arms round my defenceless physique and kissed me hungrily. "It may surprise you to know that I've gone off men completely, Peter," she whispered.

I said nothing, wondering what she had mistaken me for. I knew many girls were crazy about horses so I made an experimental whinny noise.

"You see, wherever I go out East there are thousands of sex-starved men drooling over me until I am sick of the sight of them."

"At least I'm drooling under you, darling."

"Nothing but dances and parties and night life with a bunch of spoiled officers out for all they can get."

"Despicable creatures. Thank goodness I'm not an officer."

Pamela sighed. "All I really need is a plain, ordinary, down-to-earth chap who wants to marry me for my own sake, settle down, raise a family and dig the garden."

"On a hospital ship?"

"No, Peter, but as soon as the war ends."

"How did you manage to describe me so perfectly? Mr Right—or Marine Right to be precise—is lying in your arms at this moment. Honourable mention at Cudford Horticultural Show for Early Spring Veg. Moreover, I'm a natural father, so couldn't we start that part of it now?"

"You mean you want to marry me, Peter?"

"Desperately, darling. That's why I'm proposing to you. My nightmare has always been that I may end up a lonely unwanted old bachelor in some geriatric ward."

"But you can't be more than twenty!"

"All our family worry early. My Uncle Ted insured his life directly he was old enough to have fireworks."

Pamela laughed softly. "If you really want to marry me I'll call your bluff and accept."

"Then this can be our wedding night, darling."

"There's only one tiny snag though."

"You want a white wedding in a cathedral first?"

"No, silly. It's just that there's no proof that I can trust you."

I sprang smartly to attention on my back. "You have my word as an Other Ranks and a gentleman, Pamela."

"But there are no witnesses present to hear you."

"The only witness we need is Cupid, and he's here all right—Mrs Pook!" I said emphatically, fearing, she might fetch Sister Ingram and Surgeon-Commander Mountjoy Holmes, DSO, to witness our betrothal. Never had I worked so hard for my supper or felt so woo-weary in the pursuit of love. I prayed that she would not bring up where we should live, plus the relevant mortgage problems, or produce the family album for a rundown on the guest list at the reception. Worse still, I had to keep one eye on the porthole as a pre-dawn check because it was vital I returned to Piccadilly under cover of darkness. Yet I experienced a tremor of excitement to think I was the only man on Loyota Atoll to become engaged—and against ridiculous odds at that. I reflected that if the news leaked to Lieutenant Titterton it would hardly flood his soul with ecstasy to the point where he would award me the Sword of Honour. Fortunately I was too large for midget submarines, but he had hinted previously that my big feet would make excellent mine-detectors.

Pamela snuggled into me in a most alarming manner. "Are you a Roman Catholic, darling?"

"Are you, dear?" Religion wasn't going to stand in my way tonight. In the past I had already been an Angel of Detroit, a Primitive Protomartyr and an Elected Brother of Truth. I had learned how girls brought up in these strict sects did not so much make love as explode in one's arms.

"No, Peter—I'm a Protestant."

"So am I. And I can prove it." I showed her the instant burial identity disc stamped with my name, rank, number and religion. "See, Pamela, the Marines say I'm C/E—Church of England. What's more, I'm a bachelor of Cudford Parish in the county of Cudfordshire. Shoes size 10, shirt 17 and suit 44."

"Do you want a family, Peter?"

"Of course, dear—provided we don't leave it till we're too old."

"I want eight at least."

"We'll call the first one Patience, that's for sure."

"Or Dawn."

"Please don't mention that word, dear," I said, automatically checking the porthole. Surely she didn't think I had come to visit her on a week's leave?

Pamela sighed happily. "My word, Peter, you are extremely affectionate on such short acquaintance. Can you tell me what your birth sign is?"

"What is yours, darling?" Knowing from experience how many women let the Zodiac guide their lives I was quite an expert on astrology, gaining most of my knowledge from the romantic magazines which every man should read if he is to compete in the love game.

"I'm a Pisces," Pamela giggled.

"What an extraordinary coincidence, dear—I happen to be Taurus the Bull. Everyone knows how Taurus is the ideal partner for a Pisces. Fate obviously made us for each other so don't let's waste another second." I said this with some feeling because birth signs can lead to palmistry, tea-leaves and tarot cards, not to mention a seance for two. Only last year Sandra Newbolt had produced a crystal ball at the

156

critical moment, with the result that she had seen herself as an unmarrried mother and I was chased from the house.

"Yes, Peter, Taurus and Pisces do go well together."

"Taurus likes to charge at his woman on the spot, dear."

"You see, I'm old-fashioned in some ways. I want a long romantic courtship with flowers, valentines and all that sort of thing."

"And you shall have it, darling—the true Victorian courtship spread out over minutes. I must be back at base before daybreak."

Pamela mowed my cheeks with tiny kisses to show me she understood. "War is a terrible thing, sweetheart," she whispered.

I agreed whole-heartedly. "Sure is, dear. Look what it's done to me. We Marines are men of iron, despising the lusts of the flesh, impervious to the needs of sex, yet I lay here a human wreck desperate for the love of a woman this instant, without delay, now."

As I spoke I pointed to myself in case she thought I was discussing a hypothetical situation concerning war and its effect upon the Ancient Greeks.

"So, you naughty boy, you want your prize before you have run the race," Pamela giggled.

"If I ran a race right now I'd never live to receive the prize."

"Are you sure the prize itself won't kill you, Peter?"

"Let me take my chance and die happy." I was beginning to think that before the war this girl must have been one of those journalists who set quizzes in magazines.

"Shall I put the light out, Peter?"

"If we don't hurry up it won't make any difference. We'll be able to sunbathe."

"Come to me, my wonderful husband and lover. . . ."

Just as I was obeying her order the bell rang so loudly and with such insistence that I leapt on top of Pamela with fright, suffering from severe palpitation of the heart. It was the thought-destroying peal such as is used in fire-stations to alert the brigade, and in case you wondered if it concerned you it was amplified just above your head through the Tannoy system.

"What is that—time for breakfast?" I shouted at Pamela.

"Emergency Boat Drill!" she shrieked. "We've been torpedoed!"

"Torpedoed!"

"We get one every week in case we're torpedoed. Hurry!"

Pamela was literally throwing her clothes on so I followed suit. "We have to muster all patients on A deck opposite their correct lifeboat. Oh dear, what a time to choose!"

"Shall I hide?"

"You can't. They search every cabin before the ship sinks. That terrible bell won't stop ringing until the muster has been checked."

"Shall I come with you?"

"Then we'd be one over, Peter. Can you escape through the porthole?"

"The porthole!"

I put my head out of the porthole to check for height. In the gloom it seemed like a hundred feet down to the water. "You must jump!" Pamela screamed above the bell. "Your only chance or we shall both be ruined!"

"If I jump this height I shan't be ruined—I'll be killed!"

"Hang from the rim first—that will reduce it by six feet."

As I was sliding through the porthole there came a staccato rapping on the door, accompanied by a shrill female voice shouting, "Hurry, Nurse Birkett—muster your patients at Boat Station 18 immediately!"

"Coming, Sister Ingram!"

These were the last words I heard because they coincided with a tremendous shove on my backside which sent me head first through the porthole like the launching of a torpedo. I felt my body turn over as it fell through space, until eventually I hit the sea more or less diagonally. Once again I wondered if I should ever stop sinking, and I imagined I saw the keel of the *Panacea* as a black silhouette. I recall thinking to myself how this was the ultimate brush-off by a girl, then I was clawing my way to the surface for air.

Hugging the ship's hull I swam to the landing-gangway where the Carbo was moored. Hearing the shouting of orders high above me as Boat Drill went on, I executed a very smart operation. I started the Carbo and reversed along the line of the hull, clearing the ship by the stern where the chances of being spotted were remote. I continued to sail on this course until I had put a safe distance between the *Panacea* and the Carbo. Then, with the faint glow heralding dawn on the eastern horizon, I headed for Piccadilly Island and sanctuary.

With superb cunning I steered on the curve of a great arc in the lagoon, not only to keep my distance from the *Panacea* but also to approach Piccadilly from the eastern extremity—again to cut down risk of detection.

When the sweep of the curve was taking me almost parallel to the western shore of Kensington Island something happened which I dreaded. It was one item from a long list of dreads, and it came in the shape of a small launch which purred out to me from Kensington itself. My heart sank and I prayed the Carbo would not follow suit.

After the launch had circled me once, the sole occupant called out, "Avast there and follow me to shore!"

Immediately I recognized the voice of Corporal Poster, a Regular Marine who knew all about the sea and never tired of avasting and belaying and heaving-to and all the other jargon essential for manning boats. "I can't, Corporal," I yelled back. "I'm making for Piccadilly on a special mission."

"Turn a-port and follow me or I'll sink you—like this."

Corporal Poster steered expertly at the beam of the Carbo, so that the stem of his bow gently nudged the top of my gunwale, causing me to ship a little water. "My oath, it's Pook!" he exclaimed as I surrendered without further resistance. "What you doing at sea in that . . . what the 'ell is it . . . a floating Jeep?"

I felt too miserable to reply as I followed my captor to the beach, where we were soon joined by Sergeant Vile— an NCO with so much Service tradition soaked in him that back home his wife had to report to him before shopping and say, "Proceeding ashore on the next liberty boat for victualling and dhobi. Estimated Time of Arrival back to base 1200 hours. All ashore who's going ashore!"

Sergeant Vile fetched Lieutenant Tudor, who drew me aside for cross-examination while his Sergeant and Corporal swarmed over and under the Carbo like two hungry mice.

"What game are you up to, Pook?" Lieutenant Tudor inquired.

"I'm not allowed to tell the enemy anything except my name, rank and number, sir," I replied smartly.

"Listen, idiot, the Japanese are the enemy, not me. I'm one of your own officers, so you have to divulge the lot.

For a start,where have you been?"

"Night trials, sir, testing the Carbo."

Lieutenant Tudor chuckled. "So that's what it's called, eh? Lieutenant Titterton's secret weapon. Well, we're taking a good close look at the tub right now. That must have been the unidentified craft Sergeant Vile spotted approaching the *Panacea* at 0127 hours. Have you been sneaking out to the hospital ship, Pook?"

"What would I want out there, sir?"

"Well, I don't expect you went for a dental check. By what I remember of the dance you went for a Nurse Birkett check instead. Any luck?"

"I've been spoken for, sir," I admitted, thinking how unfair it was that this man should be psychic as well as brilliant.

"Do you mean engaged?"

"Yes, sir. Engaged to be married to Nurse Birkett."

For once Lieutenant Tudor was surprised. "Good heavens! She must be . . . well, never mind that now. You realize you cannot wed in a combat zone without your Commanding Officer's permission? Fine thing if the Japs attacked us while we were all attending a white wedding."

"I'll just have to wait, sir."

"Wait! You may never live to see it, Pook. Driving a top secret vehicle, boarding an out-of-bounds ship, getting engaged on active service—you're really in the manure this time!"

"And sinking fast, sir," I admitted wretchedly, wondering if he knew about my losing Lieutenant Titterton's personal Jeep in the sea.

"You appreciate this is a court-martial job with Colonel Tank and rifles at dawn."

"As bad as that, sir?"

Suddenly Lieutenant Tudor lowered his head and went extremely sad. "Your main consolation will be that you did not make Nurse Birkett a widow—yet we shall miss you, Pook."

"At such short range, sir? Surely my own Section won't form the firing-squad?" The ridiculous thought entered my mind that if Honners, Dennis Long and Tilty Slant made up the firing-squad I should only be wounded. Perhaps under such circumstances I could claim a disability pension. Dennis had already proved that his sole hope of hitting any target was to charge at it with fixed bayonet.

Lieutenant Tudor left me for a moment while he conferred with Sergeant Vile and Corporal Poster, who were showing him notes and diagrams they had made on a clip-board as they searched the Carbo. Eventually Lieutenant Tudor returned to me, standing with feet astride and neck stuck out. "I'm going to stick my neck out, Pook," he explained.

"I can see you have already, sir," I replied puzzledly.

"I'm going to stick my neck out and do an extremely foolish thing." Surely he wasn't going to bite me like an angry swan?

"I'm going to pretend I never caught you tonight and know nothing of your escapade. In short, I'm going to release you."

My heart leapt with joy. "You're an officer and a gentleman, sir!" I gasped incredulously.

"There is only one condition, Pook. That you return to base immediately and mention nothing of your exploit to a living soul—but particulallly not to Lieutenant Titterton, understand?"

"I'm the last person on earth to blab, sir. Wild horses, etcetera."

"Good. If anybody—particularly Lieutenant Titterton should learn of your crimes I personally will see that you are shot."

"The Carbo is top secret anyway, sir. Mum's the word."

"Top secret indeed! Our lips are sealed, your lips are sealed—no-one will ever know."

"It will go down as one of the great mysteries of the war, sir."

"Exactly, Pook. Just forget the whole unfortunate business."

"Instant amnesia, sir."

"Now be off with you before daylight. Good luck to you and Nurse Birkett."

"Wedding-cake for under your pillow, sir—I won't forget."

I drove down the beach into the sea hardly daring to believe my luck. I had always admired Lieutenant Tudor as a brilliant tactician but now I knew he possessed a heart of gold, being so impressed by my love affair with Pamela against hopeless odds that his romantic nature had prompted him to let me off scot-free. In fact it was the first time I had ever experienced manifestations of love in a Royal Marine officer, whose mode of training demanded that Cupid lay riddled with his own darts. Honners went even further, referring to Lieutenant Titterton as 'That enlisted flunkey who has exchanged the pen for the sword without noticing the difference.' But now my attitude was changed, for I saw Pamela and me walking from the church under a bridal arch of bren-guns held aloft by my loving officers while they showered us with improvised confetti of leave-chits.

As I sailed south towards Piccadilly Island the current began to give me some trouble. The set of the tide was carrying the Carbo to port no matter how I steered to starboard. This tide versus tiller resulted in my progressing on a diagonal course, but there was no doubt that I was being swept towards the eastern extremity of Piccadilly Island to Wopping Old Stairs in fact.

After ten minutes I realized that I was not going to make even Wopping Old Stairs. I was being washed out of the lagoon through the channel between Kensington Island and Piccadilly Island, just as our bumboat had been caught previously. Far beyond the gap I perceived the beautiful sight I dreaded, for the first segment of the sun was bulging out of the ocean like the hump of an enormous golden whale. Momentarily I was entranced by the grandeur of the spectacle, actually feeling the eastward roll of this tiny ball we call Earth as it hangs in the universe invisibly chained to its master the Sun.

Then I plunged back to reality as I fought to reach land, spinning the wheel in the hope of gaining the southern tip of Kensington Island instead. But the tidal-race was too powerful, for I was carried through the centre of the channel at some twenty knots, my screw and tiller all but useless. I felt angry and desperate at the way Fate had treated me, but above all I experienced utter loneliness as I was spewed out into the vasty ocean. Even the company of Honners would have been some consolation upon these chartless waters.

Moreover, it was impossible to drown in Honners' company because he had assured me that God wanted him safely back in Cudford to administer his estate, and that He would brook no interference from the Royal Marines or the Japanese Fleet in their efforts to drown him before then.

Honners also told me he went to sleep by counting sheep—counting his own sheep back at Cudford in case one of them had been poached, and then counted every other item on the Pilkington-Goldberg parklands for the same reason.

But at that moment, as I drifted helplessly out into the mighty waste of the Indian Ocean, Honners was fast asleep in his tent, smirking smugly as he dreamed of the fertile acres adjoining Cudford Hall awaiting his personal attention.

ELEVEN

As I was flushed through the strait like a matchbox along a storm gutter the Carbo slewed crazily in response to the wheel, so that at one point I was actually sailing stern first. In extreme emergency logical thinking becomes almost impossible, yet instinct seems to take over. I noticed that I was slightly closer to Piccadilly Island than to Kensington, whereupon I struggled to keep the Carbo bow on to the rising sun in the hope that, once through the tidal race, I might gain the lee of Piccadilly and have sufficient power to reach the island in slack water.

Once clear of the lagoon I tried to veer southwards very gradually, lest I ship any more seas over the low gunwale, yet it must have been two miles before I was sufficiently out of the tide to attempt the home run in the shelter of Piccadilly Island. Even then I wondered if the Carbo had enough power to make headway, and little means of knowing if I was succeeding or merely drifting astern.

Yet soon there was no doubt in my mind that I was gaining against the tide because the island grew bigger before me. Then a most extraordinary thing happened. The Carbo rose nearly a foot and I could feel the wheels grounding on something hard as the vehicle stopped. Thinking I had hit an offshore rock I engaged the four-wheeled drive, whereupon the Carbo lumbered forward through the water as though covering rough terrain on land. I could scarcely believe what was happening, for the island was still the best part of a mile off. The mystery was solved when the sun was high enough for me to see below the surface—I was actually driving the Carbo in low gear across the barrier reef that surrounded the entire atoll. I bumped and lurched in this fashion until I reached the beach itself, Brighton Beach as it had been christened, which I knew well. I was safe at last.

Safe from the elements that is, but certainly not safe from Lieutenant Titterton because from this point it was not possible to drive any vehicle round the shore back to the Motor Transport base, nor could one penetrate the hinterland. Walk yes, but drive no. Palm trees grew everywhere like weeds, many of them soaring diagonally over the beach itself, and for good measure their fallen companions lay scattered like giant matches from a giant's box. Even a tank could not have made it.

There was only one course of action left me, which was to abandon the Carbo, then return to base on foot in the hope that my absence had not been detected. Lieutenant Titterton could work out for himself how his precious Carbo came to be parked on Brighton Beach—and come to that, how to get it back to the MT sheds. At least he might be grateful that it had reappeared and was undamaged.

Just as I was about to practise our jungle training by melting into the undergrowth, a voice rang out so loud and bugle-like that it had to be Honners. "Who goes there? Friend or foe? Halt or I fire!"

As Honners ran towards me I could discern Lieutenant Titterton far behind him. I halted but Honners continued to shriek his commands till they echoed round the island.

"Hands up! Don't move or I fire! Name, rank and number!"

"All right, Honners, I've surrendered. You haven't captured the entire Jap army."

Honners winked. "Just clearing my own yard-arm. Big trouble. Titters missed his Carbo. He knows nothing about the *Panacea* and Pamela. Nor do I, got it? He detailed me for search party so I led him here to Brighton Beach—the one place I thought you couldn't be. Think fast for once. Tell him the isolation here has driven you potty and you tried to end it all in the 'ogwash . . . . Prisoner, SHUN!"

Lieutenant Titterton arrived red of face and wild eyed, like a man pursued by a bee swarm. He ignored me temporarily as he flung himself into the Carbo, starting it, testing it and examining it simultaneously.

"Gone off his rocker," Honners informed me privately. "He ran about the MT sheds like a squirrel with a nervous breakdown who's lost its nuts. Then he followed me here as if he thought he was a kangaroo. Probably fits coming on. I thoroughly enjoyed it."

Lieutenant Titterton bounded over to me trembling and spluttering. All he could articulate was "Yes, Pook?"

"The Carbo is safe and sound, sir," I barked smartly, figuring it wisest to give him the good news first. "I desperately wanted to be your driver, sir, so in a mad moment of ambition I foolishly took the Carbo without a soul knowing about it to see if I could circumnavigate the island and surprise you, sir. I was trying to display initiative to help you and our Section, sir, but now I realize I went too far, sir. Your own example and leadership made me too eager for promotion, sir—I should have obtained your permission first of course, but I wanted to show you how your training has inspired me, sir."

"The sun has sent him off his onion, sir," Honners said. "Shall I handcuff him before he goes delirious? He doesn't know what he's saying."

Lieutenant Titterton seemed mollified and impressed by my explanation. "Go on, Pook," he snapped.

"Well, sir, your marvellous intensive Combat Training Course has made a new man of me. I now have this irresistible urge to pull my weight under your leadership to make us the top Section. In short, sir, you have accomplished the impossible—you have inspired me!"

"He's mad, sir!" Honners intervened. "I've seen it coming like a boil on your bottom. He's a gibbering wreck. Doesn't know what he's saying. Don't listen to such lies."

"Silence, Honners," Lieutenant Titterton ordered. His eyes were slits of Machiavellian cunning because he could perceive what ordinary men could not. "Tell me exactly how you came to be stranded on Brighton Beach, Pook."

I saluted smartly to let him know I was not only inspired but also hypnotized by his steely gaze. "Well, sir, when I rounded Wopping Old Stairs point the tide was so strong that I was swept out of the lagoon for nearly two miles in cable lengths or nautical knots, as we say at sea. Avast there, I said to myself, belay and heave-to while you remember what Lieutenant Titterton taught you to do in an emergency like this."

"Excellent precept, Pook. Proceed."

"It was just as though you were by my side, sir, advising and encouraging me. I decided to wear short, ease the helm and gradually busk to starboard so as to gain the lee of Piccadilly, sir," I barked, giving him the nautical chat for effect.

"And then?"

"Once I was snugged clear of the tide and fetching up in slack sea room I was able to stand free, all afluking, and close with the land. Then, some halfway, an amazing thing happened."

"You ran out of nautical terms and discovered you

weren't a three-masted clipper?"

"No, sir—the Carbo rose a foot in the water and lay-to. She had grounded on the outer reef. I was astonished to find I could change into four-wheeled drive and trundle through the water for nearly a nautical mile until I reached this beach, sir."

"Fantastic!" Lieutenant Titterton cried. "By your foolhardy escapade you have unwittingly solved my most difficult tactical problem. Brighton Beach is considered impregnable because even invasion-barges cannot negotiate the barrier reef—yet now we learn empirically that it is vulnerable to my Carbo. Wonderful!"

"But surely we don't want to attack ourselves, sir?"

Lieutenant Titterton pursed his lips and smiled esoterically. "Exactly, Pook. But in the major exercise ahead —Exercise Mad Dogs—we are to attack Kensington Island. Lieutenant Tudor believes his outer shore at Blackpool Beach is similarly impregnable—yet I can breach it with my Carbo. He doesn't even know I have been entrusted by Colonel Tank to develop the combat potential of this exciting new mode of marine transport. I shall lead you to VICTORY!"

"What a splendid idea—you attacking Kensington Island all on your own," Honners observed.

"Oh no, Honners. You won't grasp the grand strategy of my masterplan, but I personally shall spearhead the attack in the Carbo, with Pook as my helmsman. Lieutenant Tudor will be taken unawares from the rear, outwitted, outflanked, overrun—in short, the poor devil will suffer humiliating defeat at my hands. Victory will be mine!—I mean our Section's."

"Hooray," Honners groaned.

Lieutenant Titterton bored his eyes into me with the technique he employed for hypnotizing his troops, so I went glassy-eyed under his spell. "There is only one condition, Pook—and you, Honners—not a soul must know about our meeting today or the journey you have undertaken in the Carbo. Secrecy is vital to the success of my stratagem. One single leak and it's rifles at dawn under the Articles of War. Do I make myself absolutely clear, men?"

"Our lips are sealed," Honners agreed, noticing that I was incapable of answering under the influence of our officer's dominating gaze. All I could think about was my pledge to Lieutenant Tudor only hours before which seemed to clash harshly with this new promise to Lieutenant Titterton. My main worry was which officer would shoot me first, whether we won or I lost the battle. Another nightmare was the possibility of Pamela contacting Lieutenant Titterton to claim me as her bridegroom.

My nimble brain froze at the thought, for it was vital to keep my visits to the *Panacea* and Kensington Island secret. One leak could spark off a chain of inquiry that would be impossible to extinguish. I decided I was moderately safe at the moment, so my best plan would be to bask in Lieutenant Titterton's unaccustomed approval while it was going.

"So you want to be my pilot, Pook?" Lieutenant Titterton remarked thoughtfully.

"I'd rather drive the Carbo, sir. I didn't even know we had a plane."

"I mean pilot the Carbo to help me spearhead the attack. You see, *Remplir on Strategy* insists that surprise is the greatest factor in battle."

"It sure is, sir." If this was true then my surprise for

Lieutenant Titterton should win any war.

"Remplir states we must strike the enemy as follows: One, unexpectedly; two, violently; three, where he least anticipates it—and if possible, four, *by methods unknown to him.*"

"That won't be easy, sir."

"Note how, in World War I, the Germans were demoralized and routed by our use of the first tanks."

"But we haven't got any tanks, sir."

Lieutenant Titterton sighed patiently. "Hell's bells, Pook, you aren't exactly another Duke of Wellington!"

"No sir, but you are," I replied on cue.

Lieutenant Titterton smiled modestly and assumed his favourite pose of a dismounted Duke of Wellington in shorts. "Quite so, quite so, but you are showing a little more promise than hitherto. The point I am making is that Lieutenant Tudor is *completely unaware of my Carbo*—vide Remplir's Advantage Number Four."

"But the whole Section can't possibly squeeze into the Carbo, sir. It only holds four men at best."

"Unless we form a human pyramid," Honners suggested helpfully. "I'll sit right at the apex with my head just above water to guide you."

Lieutenant Titterton chuckled at the notion. "Leave it to me, men. I guarantee to land our entire Section on Blackpool Beach in readiness for my grand strategy. You will be amazed by the results. Exercise Mad Dogs will become a text-book classic, the ultimate in Combined Ops to destroy Lieutenant Tudor . . . I mean the enemy . . . once and for all by a single blow of unparalleled cunning and ferocity. Now dismiss and preserve absolute silence about this unofficial briefing."

The Japanese were forgotten as we buckled down to the task of defeating the real enemy—Lieutenant Tudor and his cocky Section. Never before had our preparation been so thorough or so carefully rehearsed.

Lieutenant Titterton had constructed a six-feet scale model of Kensington Island, marked with every detail necessary to its capture. We were to land by night on Blackpool Beach at Position PS. This stood for Proceed South, and was located where the barrier reef had a deep indentation, according to the Admiralty Chart, being a mere half mile broad at that point. The V of this indentation was aptly named Position V, so the mystery was how thirty armed men were to negotiate the reef from Position V to Position PS without being swept away or drowned.

From Position PS we were to march south to Position TW—Turn West—halfway down the east coast of Kensington Island, then turn inland for a direct attack on Position X, Lieutenant Tudor's main base. Thus Lieutenant Tudor would be assailed from behind his defence lines and annihilated.

Immediately he saw the model island and heard Lieutenant Titterton's plan of action Honners reported sick with tropical gout in both feet, claimed his blood had turned to uric acid and his joints were locked with sodium orates, and demanded instant treatment with aegopodium podagraria lest his toes fell off. This rare ailment reduced Honners to a hobbling wreck of a Marine who could only reach the canteen and mess with the aid of two sticks accompanied by cries of pain. He had dyed both big toes purple and wore sandals so that all might witness the prominent causes of his misery—a sight which so affected some of his comrades that they reeled in sympathy and accidentally trod on them.

The MO was less considerate than might have been expected from a physician, striking Honners' toes with his little reflex hammer and applying a hot poultice so suddenly that it was said Honners' scream could be heard throughout the seven islands of the Atoll. As a result of the treatment Honners' toes swelled up so much that the MO was forced to give him an excused-boots chit and a soothing ointment, but nothing more.

Honners was livid. "Here I am, in danger of losing both my feet, and what do I get from that qualified undertaker? Germoline and excused-boots! I suppose if they carried me into his butcher's shop riddled with machine-gun bullets he'd give me a packet of Quaker Oats to stop me leaking. Go to him with both legs shot away and you'd end up with an excused-trousers chit."

Lieutenant Titterton would have none of it, even if he did call Honners the Yellow Peril. When you have to conquer the world with thirty men every Marine is vital, including the lame and lazy. Among the new techniques we had to master was tiptoe marching, whereby the entire Section rose six inches on the command like a corps de ballet and glided silently along in what Sergeant Canyon called the Swan Lake Creep. If Honners cried out in pain he got hit. In addition we blacked up and wore palm leaves for camouflage, then rehearsed the final assault tactics until we had learned to move silently like a mobile hedge searching for a field to surround. But worst of all was the landing by sea.

Lieutenant Titterton's masterplan involved a 3-inch circumference rope of best manilla, buoyed every two fathoms, not by conventional cork, but by a foot-long sleeve of bamboo, chamfered at each end to reduce drag when immersed. When spliced together the final rope exceeded 170 fathoms in length.

This mass of rope and wood was meticulously coiled in the well of our landing-craft, to be paid out as the Carbo towed it ashore. We learned during practice how Lieutenant Titterton had conceived the idea of anchoring the landing-craft at Position V on the reef, then launching the Carbo and employing it to haul the rope across the reef to the shore, where it would be secured round a tree and utilized as a lifeline to enable us to pull ourselves ashore through the shallow waters right onto Blackpool Beach.

Lieutenant Titterton loved the massive coil of rope second only to the Carbo, inspecting it, fondling it, protecting it, as if he had taken up snake worship and had a monster python secreted in a floating temple. For security reasons he exercised us only at night, using Brighton Beach on our own island for realistic rehearsal, and permitting Honners to wear a lifebelt to compensate for his lack of height. After three weeks intensive training he was satisfied all was ready, every flaw ironed out, every man knew his job wherever he was at any time. Honners was warned that even if he did have blackwater fever and died his body would still be towed through the sea, dragged overland and pushed into the final attack in order to make up the requisite number of the assault party. There was no escape.

Exercise Mad Dogs began under radio silence at 1900 hours on the Monday. Beneath his palm leaves Honners was wearing the lifebelt on top of a lifejacket as a double precaution, and I happened to know that he had jettisoned the equipment from his haversack and replaced it with two football bladders—"This suicidal folly of Titters is going to be the survival of the fattest," he remarked to me. "If, through some error of judgement on his part, the sea or the sharks don't get us first, Lieutenant Tudor will. It is not my ambition to be sent home to my next-of-kin sealed in an airtight canister and labelled 'Shark containing Honners. Do not fillet or bone. Legs will follow shortly in separate shark.'"

Our big night had come at last.

TWELVE

A palm tree stood in the centre of a small banana plantation and hissed, "Right, men, this is it. Synchronize your watches."

"How do you do that?" inquired an extremely short bush potted in sandals.

"You check your watch now, idiot—19O3 hours."

"I still can't do it."

"Why not, man?"

"I haven't got a watch."

"Why haven't you got a watch, curse you, Honners?"

"The armed guard took it off me in case I hanged myself."

"You don't need a watch anyhow, being mere cannon-fodder. Sergeant Canyon and Corporal Crood, are your watches synchronized?"

"Mine says anti-magnetic, sir," Puffy replied puzzledly.

"I mean did you check it at 1903 hours?"

"Oh. Yes, sir."

"Are we all present and correct, Sergeant Canyon?"

"Yes, sir."

"Except me," Honners said. "I regret to report that I have been taken ill on the march and need immediate medical aid—preferably in England."

"We haven't started to march yet, you horrible little malingerer!" Lieutenant Titterton snapped.

"That proves I must be delirious. My thermometer registers 104 already. Blackwater fever is usually fatal anyway, so if you'll kindly step back I'll collapse in a neat pile ready for the vultures. You lot go on ahead as per schedule so I won't delay the Exercise by having to be buried first."

Lieutenant Titterton's leaves rustled with temper as he

177

parted Honners' foliage and snatched a thermometer from his mouth. "This is WAR, Honners, and if you play me up once more you'll be buried with a bullet through your skull —like this!"

We all watched delightedly as Lieutenant Titterton drew a bulky forty-five Colt and jammed it into Honners' temple. "Go on, sir, shoot his head off," Tilty cried, excited by the drama.

Lieutenant Titterton withdrew the revolver reluctantly. "I may be compelled to later under the Articles of War, but nothing must divert us from the task on hand. Sergeant, march the Section to our landing-craft."

Sergeant Canyon marched his double hedge to the beach like a portable garden for embarkation. The Carbo was swung between two davits mounted on the stern of the landing-craft, the twin Chrysler engines purred sweetly and every man took up his allotted position. We set course away from Kensington Island because Lieutenant Titterton was taking us out of the lagoon the long way round on what he designated as Route Back Door. After rounding the western extremity of our own island we passed well clear of Brighton Beach, then Wopping Old Stairs, until we stood some three miles off Blackpool Beach itself.

Our landing-craft had been camouflaged with black paint to merge with the darkness, so Lieutenant Titterton now changed course to head directly for Position V on the barrier reef. He personally took the helm from Regular Marine Duggie Drew at this stage, while Sergeant Canyon used the leadline up for'ard to pinpoint this vital spot. In addition Corporal Crood employed a kind of punt pole to feel for the reef.

When Lieutenant Titterton was satisfied by all our aids

to navigation that we had reached Position V we dropped anchor. Well drilled, we lowered the Carbo into the water from the stern davits by winch, then Lieutenant Titterton and I climbed down into it and cast off. Under my officer's eagle eye I steered for the beach, changing into four-wheeled drive directly we touched the reef. Behind us the buoyed rope was being paid out by our cable team.

All credit to Lieutenant Titterton, for the operation functioned smoothly. The Carbo eventually trundled up the beach, whereupon we selected a stout palm tree and between us we secured the rope around it.

"Success!" Lieutenant Titterton shouted in his top security whisper. "Stage 2 completed without a hitch. Now for the main landing."

Lieutenant Titterton flashed the code word Fish by means of a hooded Aldis lamp beamed precisely on the landing-craft. This was the signal to commence the run ashore. From the beach we could actually hear that the first man to come was an extremely unwilling Honners, hand-picked for his courage and to prevent his hiding in the bowels of the landing-craft. As usual on such forays, Honners had to be shoved, lifted, thrown, punched, and even kicked into action while he screamed abuse at his persuaders—from Sergeant Canyon right through to the Allied High Command.

The noise stopped abruptly the moment Honners entered the sea upside-down, closely followed by Corporal Crood, whose job it was to get Honners upright and shove him along the rope until his feet could touch bottom.

"Curse that man for breaking, silence," Lieutenant Titterton growled petulantly flashing the code word Mum for negative noise.

This signal evoked a terrible oath from out of the

darkness concerning Lieutenant Titterton's mum and what would happen to her if Honners survived drowning and was able to get his hands round her throat.

Eventually Corporal Crood got Honners to the beach, where he was spread out to drain and recover from the ordeal while the remainder of the Section negotiated the reef and hauled themselves ashore. When every man had been accounted for, Lieutenant Titterton flashed the code word Pigeon to instruct Duggie Drew to pilot the landing-craft back to Piccadilly Island.

"Good show, men," Lieutenant Titterton praised us. "Landing according to plan. Now we proceed along the coast to Point TW, where we shall reassemble for the journey inland and the main assault. Marine Marks will accompany Corporal Crood ahead of us to reconnoitre the land. We shall follow in jungle Dispersal Order. Forward to victory, men!"

As we crept through the undergrowth Honners whispered to me, "Never mind about jungle Dispersal Order, Peter just hang on to Titters so we don't get lost."

"But we're supposed to spread out to avoid detection."

"Use your loaf, Peter. How can we find Point TW in this light? It's marked by a dead crab with one claw or something equally nauseating. If Titters is so smart let him locate it, closely followed by even smarter us."

"Not a dead crab, Honners—a pile of sandbags for building an ack-ack site."

"So we tail Titters and let him do the Boy Scout tracking job."

In the jungle stillness Honners' idea seemed extremely attractive and safer, so we began to play a kind of hide-and-seek behind our officer lest he caught sight of us. But, as

Honners had pointed out, he did lead us safely to Point TW.

"Good show, Pook and Honners—first to arrive at TW assembly point," Lieutenant Titterton praised us.

"On the ball as usual, sir," I barked, saluting smartly. "Your intensive course of Orienteering has paid off with us, sir. Give me a map, compass and the stars and I'll follow you to the end of the world."

"Probably the next world," Honners added.

Soon afterwards a huge bush lumbered into our clearing—Hardy Annual Crusher, as Honners now called Sergeant Canyon, followed by various lesser varieties of evergreen. When heads had been counted Lieutenant Titterton announced that we were four bushes short. Marines Phil Trenchard and Harry Low, who formed the rearguard, had not yet arrived, but surprisingly enough our advance party of Corporal Crood and Mickey Marks were missing too.

"Curse the stupid slackers!" Lieutenant Titterton hissed, agitatedly consulting his luminous watch. "Surely they haven't overshot Point TW after all our training. I'll give them another three minutes, then they're in the rattle."

"Disgraceful!" Honners agreed. "They've let the Section down badly. I've always said that if Crood is a Corporal then I should be a General, or whoever it is who struts about a battleship's balcony wearing a cocked hat and shooting his big mouth off."

When three minutes had elapsed Lieutenant Titterton raised his right bough and announced, "That's it, men. Nothing shall endanger our schedule. They must catch us up according to Contingency Plan One. Heaven help them when I get them back to base. Forward to Point FA at the crossroads where we muster for the final assault on Lieutenant Tudor . . . I mean on the heart of the enemy's camp. Proceed in jungle Dispersal Order as before."

Our little forest melted away as if by magic, except that Honners and I advanced backwards to give Lieutenant Titterton time to go forwards.

"This is a real cushy number," Honners whispered. "Why get lost in this blessed science-fiction orchard when all you have to do is play your cards right and follow our human bloodhound?"

For once I agreed with Honners, so with commendable skill we followed the commissioned bush in front of us at a safe distance as Lieutenant Titterton progressed through the night by the aid of map and compass. Our final rendezvous was Point FA, from which the final assault on the enemy was to be mounted. Point FA was the crossroads where the little track to the gunsite from the camp crossed the main road which had been constructed along the length of the island, and was therefore the virtual centre of Kensington Island. Directly Lieutenant Titterton had established himself at Point FA Honners and I split up in order to converge upon him from opposite sides.

"Well done, men—first again," Lieutenant Titterton congratulated us. "I only wish the rest of the Section was as smart as you two."

"Nothing really, sir," I smiled modestly. "We merely follow your marvellous example. Anybody could do the same with you as their leader."

"Quite so, Pook, quite so—but where are the others? We're already six minutes behind schedule."

"Now you know where your officer material is," Honners reminded him. "Jungle Dispersal Order sure separates the men from the boys. Still, what can one expect from the lower classes? I mean, take fox-hunting, for example. Stick some nouveau riche ironmonger on a horse and he starts bawling tally-ho and looks for the fox underneath his Rolls in the carpark."

When our weary Section finally rallied at Point FA and Sergeant Canyon had counted heads we were seven men short this time, plus the four we had lost at Point TW.

"Perhaps they've gone down with malaria," Honners suggested.

"Silence, Honners," Lieutenant Titterton fumed. "Eleven men missing at the vital moment of assault. All I can muster is twenty-one men. Twenty-one men to encircle and capture the enemy! Where in hell are they, that's what I demand to know?"

Rapid interrogation revealed that no-one had any knowledge of the missing men or how they had disappeared so mysteriously.

"All my best and most experienced troops gone!" Lieutenant Titterton bewailed wretchedly.

"Take courage—I am still here," Honners reminded him.

"That's what I mean. All my regulars missing. Nothing left but the ullage, the sick, the walking wounded. How could such a thing happen to me?"

"We'll all fight twice as hard, sir—fight like forty-two men, sir," I barked, smartly saluting with my leaves.

Lieutenant Titterton winced. "About as much good to me as a pram in a convent. Surely this never happened to the Iron Duke."

"Even worse, sir. When his reinforcements arrived he said, 'I don't know what effect these men will have upon the enemy, but, by God, they terrify me.' "

Honners joined me in rallying round our officer in his

dilemma. "This is a grave emergency, such as brings out the best in every man. Do not be downhearted, remember *Per Mare Per Terram*, we are not mere squaddies, we're Royal Marines. All for one and one for all; united we stand, divided we fall. No matter what happens let every true Bootneck stand firm behind his officer, determined to do or die for England while he surrenders without delay."

Lieutenant Titterton gasped. "Do not mention that vile word in my presence, Honners. I shall surrender to Lieutenant Tudor only over my dead body."

"So you're going to do a back somersault onto a bayonet for a quick hara-kiri then?"

"Whatever I do I shall never surrender. I do not know the meaning of it."

"It means give up. It should be our motto 'He who fights and runs away lives to booze and draw his pay.' After all, it's only a bloomin' exercise. Treat it like chess. Having lost so many men you can say I resign. Very loudly in case they shoot us first. Then we can get on with the real object of the war."

"Defeating the Japanese, of course."

"No, beat it back home to Blighty in one piece."

"Silence, you horrible little traitor. I shall lead you to victory. My mind is made up. I shall redeploy our forces and attack with twenty-one men regardless of the risk. Sergeant Canyon, aux armes! Unleash the dogs of war!"

"We ain't got no dogs, sir," Crusher replied puzzledly.

Lieutenant Titterton briefed Sergeant Canyon, who in turn gave us fresh orders to fill the gaps left by our missing comrades. When our officer was satisfied that every man understood his new role he gave the command to advance for the final assault on Lieutenant Tudor's stronghold in crescent formation to ensure that every part of the perimeter would be penetrated.

Honners and I disappeared into the jungle, waited, then hurried forward so that, crescent formation or not, we should be directly behind Lieutenant Titterton. So accurate was Honners' sense of direction that after only ten minutes we accidentally bumped into our officer. In fact, Honners actually tripped over his body as Lieutenant Titterton lay in the grass surveying the land through night-glasses.

"What the devil are you doing here?" Lieutenant Titterton demanded. "Why aren't you in Extended Order as instructed?"

Without hesitation Honners replied, "It is my duty to report an emergency."

"You have contacted the enemy, Honners?"

"I have contracted Holtzenheimer's Urticaria or l'urticaire rouge."

"What in heaven's name is that? Can't you ever speak without appearing to have wedged a medical dictionary down your gullet?"

"It is a most distressing allergy. I require immediate injections of adrenalin."

"In the middle of a battle! Tell me in plain language what is wrong with you this time, apart from the obvious."

"I am a victim of Holtzenheimer's Urticaria or l'urticaire rouge—covered with it in fact."

"That should look good on your death certificate," Lieutenant Titterton laughed mirthlessly. "Now get into your position for the big attack."

"I have already been attacked by this terrible allergy nettle-rash in the vulgar patois."

"Nettle-rash! Not surprising either—your tatty camouflage is full of nettles. just look at it."

Honners' prominent nostrils flared. "For your information Holtzenheimer's Urticaria or l'urticaire rouge is caused by eating shellfish, violent emotional shock or contact with a horse. Lately I have been compelled to eat shell-fish until I am often unable to stop myself walking sideways like a crab, and when I experience yet another violent emotional shock—*videlicet* being flung into the sea upside-down from a barge this evening—my eyeballs seem to rise upwards on two stalks. As to contact with a horse— that delightful ungulate mammal Equus Caballus of the family Equidae—the Royal Marines have gone one better by forcing me to eat one under the guise of corned beef. Hence the rash-ridden wreck you see before you now."

Lieutenant Titterton rose to his feet and fixed Honners with his Duke of Wellington eye. "Get to combat stations this instant, Honners, or I shall have no option but to cure you permanently with this Royal College of Surgeons' instant euthanasia revolver. We attack in seven minute— and that's an order. You too, Pook. Get your patient mobile at once."

Honners and I hurried off into the night after such a threat, yet Honners still led me on a circular route so we were once again behind Lieutenant Titterton. "Attacking Lieutenant Tudor and Co. is no joke, Peter," he explained into my ear. "We've lost a third of the Section already and that was merely on the journey. The actual attack will be all hell let loose, so Titters can go in first while we wait and see if it's worth the risk following him."

"But we're supposed to support him on his left flank, Honners."

"We'll support him on his left flank all right provided

he's winning. If not, we'll support him on his back flank by covering his rear. I'm not getting my head knocked off by Tudor and his Glasgow razor gang just for some potty exercise. I don't suppose the Allied Nations will be defeated by the Axis Powers just because you and I turn up five minutes late for tonight's slaughter."

"Well, I'm going in anyway, Honners."

"Bravo! You follow Titters, then I'll follow you. That way I can double-check on the opposition and be in the best position to lead the retreat."

As I dashed through the enemy lines during the final assault the strange feeling assailed me that friend and foe were both conspicuous by their absence. There seemed to be nobody supporting me, nor did anyone appear to be opposing me. When I ran into Lieutenant Tudor's base I discovered Lieutenant Titterton already there, flourishing his revolver and shouting a great deal about victory being his, followed by several rhetorical questions as to the where-abouts of his own men. He appeared to have taken the stronghold single-handed, racing bravely in at the head of his invisible troops. In fact, until I arrived he was com-pletely on his own.

"Ah, there you are, Pook," he shouted when I saluted. "Victory is mine . . . ours, rather. Well done."

"Where is the enemy, sir?" I inquired, just as Honners charged recklessly into the camp with fixed-bayonet, though I perceived the bayonet to be fixed to the end of his arm because he had lost his rifle during the landing by sea.

"The enemy has obviously fled, Pook," Lieutenant Titterton said confidently, searching for it under several tents which lay flattened on the ground.

"Strikes me everybody has fled—including our lot,"

Honners observed. "We've won three nil."

"Where is everyone, sir? Surely Sergeant Canyon and the others should be here by now?"

"Perhaps we got the date wrong and should have attacked tomorrow night," Honners remarked.

Lieutenant Titterton was growing agitated. "Didn't you see any of our fellows in the jungle, either of you?"

"Didn't meet a soul except you," Honners volunteered.

"Haven't glimpsed the enemy either, sir," I added. "Are you certain this is the right island?"

Lieutenant Titterton did not answer. With the aid of his torch he was examining the ground around us like a leafy Sherlock Holmes, pausing every so often to scrutinize something more closely. I gathered from his exclamations that these were no ordinary finds.

"Great gophers!—a Japanese helmet and a sword! Here's one of their forage-caps too!"

"Japs!" Honners snapped incredulously.

"Close on me, men," our officer cried but it was too late because we had already closed on him as tightly as possible at the mention of the dreaded foe from the East, like a small rugby scrum.

"I have unravelled the mystery, and the news is not good, he announced dramatically. "A Japanese raiding party has obviously been here before us, hence the absence of Lieutenant Tudor and his Section."

"And the absence of our Section, sir," I whispered. "We must be the only three left alive."

"Keep calm, Pook. There is no need to embrace me like a lover, with Honners as your jealous rival."

"They don't take prisoners," Honners groaned, "so we can't even surrender like gentlemen."

"They must have attacked the island during our Exercise and captured everybody," Lieutenant Titterton decided.

"Except us three, sir. We must have slipped through their net by accident."

"Let's take to the trees and hang upside-down like giant bats," Honners suggested urgently.

"Hush!" Lieutenant Titterton warned. "What was that?"

"A faint cry for help, sir. It came from behind that Jeep."

"Exactly, men. It may be a trap. A Japanese soldier calling for help."

"Perhaps the word *Help* is Japanese for 'Lay down your arms and surrender because you are surrounded, outnumbered and about to be shot,'" Honners said.

"Or one of Lieutenant Tudor's men who was left for dead," I suggested.

Lieutenant Titterton stiffened. "We'll take no chances and operate Plan S. Spread out in a triangle, each man covering, the other with Pook at the apex. Honners covers Pook and I cover Honners. Go ahead to investigate, Pook— secure in the knowledge that you are doubly covered by supporting fire."

"But Honners has lost his rifle."

"Advance immediately, idiot. I have you fully covered."

"Comprehensive or third party only?" Honners inquired.

As I edged forward towards the Jeep I distinctly heard the cry for help repeated—apparently from a man in great pain. I glanced back at Honners and noticed something completely new. He was wearing Red Cross armbands on either sleeve. Before I could comment on this device he hissed at me, "Hurry up, you big coward—our lives may depend on you. If it moves shoot it."

THIRTEEN

Why, I asked myself, was Honners never able to give me supporting fire in a crisis? Tonight he had lost his rifle, on Crete he claimed that the shop had sold him the wrong size cartridges. In North Africa he purported to have caught Ménière's Disease, with its sudden attacks of giddiness and ringing of a high musical note, causing him to shoot wildly to the accompaniment of church bells.

I lay on my belly flatter than a snake and oozed towards the Jeep, trying to take my mind off sudden death by recalling how Sergeant Canyon had received the news about Ménière's Disease by advising Honners not to go out with Ménière while he was still infectious. In Burma Honners had been expressly forbidden to give anybody supporting fire because his gas-mask had steamed up and Lieutenant Titterton had received a bullet which fortunately ricocheted off his helmet.

"Help!" came the cry once more, now a moan.

"Where are you—friend or foe?"

"Friend, here under the Jeep. Is that Peter?"

"This is Honners," I replied cunningly to check his reply.

"Don't muck about, Peter. This is Stickers—Corporal Poster."

"Advance and be recognized, Stickers."

"I'll do my best. I'll roll out from under the Jeep."

Lieutenant Titterton ran forward, blinding Corporal Poster by thrusting the torch right in his face. "Hell's bells, it is Corporal Poster!" he confirmed. "Where is Lieutenant Tudor and the rest of your Section?"

"I thought you would have known, sir."

"Known what, man?"

"About the surprise attack by the Japanese during our Exercise. Didn't Colonel Tank radio you, sir?"

"This is the first I've heard about it, Corporal. Are you seriously wounded?"

Corporal Poster put a hand to his bandaged head. "Nothing, sir, just a stray bullet grazed my temple. That's why I am unable to stand up and salute you, sir."

"Good grief! Where is Lieutenant Tudor?"

"I don't know, sir. We were all set for your attack on this base when the Japanese landed further along the beach and encircled us. We had no chance, sir. There was about a thousand of them. I escaped by sheer good luck, sir. A bullet stunned me, I fell under the Jeep and in the dark the Japs missed me."

"Then who bandaged you up?"

"I managed to do it myself, sir."

"Good show, Corporal. When did Lieutenant Tudor receive the signal about the invasion?"

"Not until the Japs had landed, sir. That's how we knew it wasn't you, sir."

"Did he give any special orders?"

"He said to hold out as long as possible sir, and make our way to Piccadilly Island if we could. He said that would be the rallying point until we could summon support from the Navy."

Lieutenant Titterton's eyes flashed. "That's it! All hands to Piccadilly Island without a moment's delay. The question is how to get there."

"We have one slender chance, sir," Corporal Poster replied. "The Japs have taken all our sea transport but Lieutenant Tudor always kept an outboard dinghy hidden in case of emergency—I doubt if the Japs found that."

"Where is it located, Corporal?"

"I can show you, sir. At the southern extremity of this island, camouflaged under a pile of coconut husks. Only Sergeant Vile and me were in the know about it from Lieutenant Tudor, sir."

Lieutenant Titterton smiled for the first time. "An excellent officer that. I am glad to see he has profited by my dictum never to burn one's bridges. Our immediate problem is the disposition of the Japanese forces."

"They seemed to move off in a northerly direction so we should be all right, sir. We'll travel south, keeping clear of the beach and the track—it's only about a mile and a half."

"Splendid, Corporal. Given a minimum of luck we should embark well within the hour. Are you fit enough to accompany us?"

"Pretty good, sir. Anything is better than staying here alone."

"That's settled then. We'll move off without delay because time is precious in a situation like this. Corporal Poster will lead the way, I shall follow, then Honners, with Pook as rearguard."

"Couldn't we travel in a group just this once, sir?" I begged our officer. "If we linked arms we wouldn't be picked off one by one like the rest of our chaps must have been."

"Advance as I say, Pook," Lieutenant Titterton commanded sharply. "This is not the Palais Glide, nor do Royal Marines pass through dangerous territory locked in each other's arms or carrying their less courageous comrades."

Despite our officer's orders Honners kept right on his heels, while I followed Honners even closer. I noticed that

Honners was wearing the Red Cross armbands on either sleeve and had long lost his rifle. I questioned him about the matter in whispers.

"Stretcher-bearer," he hissed. "In case we get captured by the Nips. My only regret is that back at camp I have the complete outfit for a Regimental Chaplain, Church of England."

"It takes two to carry a stretcher. Have you got a spare pair of armbands for me?"

"Sorry, chum. Every man for himself in war."

"Give me one of yours then. One each is enough."

"Tell them you're a Conscientious Objector."

"Conscientious Objector! Dressed to kill like this? Rifle, bayonet, ammunition and hand-grenades—one of Churchill's Butchers. Ivan the Terrible claiming to be a nun!"

Honners sniggered. "Use your loaf, Peter. Stickers is completely unarmed, Titters has one revolver and I've accidentally lost everything. You're the only one armed to the teeth, but if the Japs attack us we shan't be able to lay down what you might call a devastating curtain of fire to wipe out a thousand men or more. So my advice to you is ditch everything, then if Titters decides to fight to the last man we'll disappear into the bush and make sure the last man is him."

"But the Japs will kill us anyway, Honners."

"Not if you listen to me. If we're ambushed we'll nip quietly off to a bullet-free zone in the jungle while Titters gets sieved up with lead, then we'll double back to Tudor's base. I know where his medical stores are, so we'll grab a stretcher and rush about looking for a body to park on it."

"But I haven't got any Red Cross armbands."

Honners felt in his pocket. "I'm a fool to do it but I'll

sell you my reserve pair for a fiver. Pay me later when we're in a Jap prisoner-of-war camp. I was going to wear these on my legs."

Gratefully I slipped the armbands on underneath my camouflage, wondering what Lieutenant Titterton would think if he knew he was being supported by two unarmed medical orderlies. Corporal Poster led us unerringly to the tip of the island without incident, halting at a pile of coconut husks. These he removed by heaving off a camouflage net which lay underneath, revealing the dinghy he had promised. An outboard engine was there too, sealed in a canvas bag. Hardly daring to believe our luck we hauled the boat to the water's edge and secured the motor over the stern. Two pulls on the cord brought the outboard to life, then Corporal Poster headed into the lagoon for Piccadilly Island, without lights.

Lieutenant Titterton took command at this stage as though he was on the bridge of a destroyer. "Nice work, Corporal. So far so good. Directly we are close enough I shall take advantage of the tide to gain the shore in silence. I know the exact spot to land which will enable us to approach our base unobserved."

"Thank you, sir," Corporal Poster replied. "I am rather done in, so now I'll relax with your permission. Good luck, sir."

Honners whispered to me, "We'll be better off on our home ground, Peter. We know it so well that I may be able to sneak into camp and grab my Chaplain's outfit. Always fancied myself as a Padre. If the Japs are in the vicinity you can tend Titters' wounds while I give him the last rites."

"But we're supposed to fight the Japs, Honners."

"Not when it's five thousand to one, matey. That's the

time to become a non-combatant."

At approximately a hundred yards from the beach Lieutenant Titterton issued orders to the engine-room of our tiny craft to cut the motor so we could land quietly. Then, all crouching as though entering a tunnel, we made for the forest cover. Here we grouped tightly around our officer for instructions.

"Now men, you all know where we are."

"In Queer Street," Honners said.

"We are three hundred yards west of our base. We shall disperse as before and approach camp with utmost caution lest it is in the hands of the Japanese. If that should be the case return here immediately."

"Shall I stay here and wait for you then?" Honners inquired.

"You will be well advised to rendezvous with the rest of us, Honners. Colonel Tank is probably awaiting us. Forward, men."

Honners and I dispersed in our customary fashion of going round in a circle to get behind Lieutenant Titterton. Corporal Poster hurried inland as ordered but almost at once I heard him give a muffled cry for help. Thinking his wound had taken its toll, Honners and I ran towards him but he had disappeared without trace.

"The blasted place is haunted!" Honners exclaimed.

"The Japs must be here too—they've whipped poor old Stickers into the night. Better catch up with Titters and warn him."

Honners shook his head. "Let him go on in front as our mine-detector. If he's OK so are we. If he gets captured we can double back. Give me the slightest chance and I'm finding our tent for the Chaplain's outfit."

"Then let's link arms for safety, Honners."

"All right, but if they grab you don't imagine I'm coming with you. The only survivor of this campaign could well be a small Church of England Padre."

We hurried off through the undergrowth until we were able to keep Lieutenant Titterton in our sights as he approached the perimeter of the camp. The whole scene appeared to be deserted and unnaturally silent—so frightening that the phenomenon of horripilation seemed to be making my hair stand on end and pushing my helmet over my eyes.

When Lieutenant Titterton lay down to survey the camp from close quarters Honners began to shed his leafy camouflage. "It all looks empty up front, Peter," he explained, "so I'm going to chance it and make a run for our tent."

"You must be crazy, Honners. The Japs may be lying in wait."

"They wouldn't bother to do that just for Titters and two stretcher-bearers. Once I can don the vicar's gear I can even pass you off as my curate. Believe me, it's our best bet."

Before I could protest further Honners crept off to the right of Lieutenant Titterton in order to gain the rear of the camp where our tent was situated. Feeling now completely exposed and lonely I followed a course roughly half way between that of Honners and Lieutenant Titterton. This route brought me so close to the camp that I could glimpse our tent just as Honners slunk inside it.

Without warning the tent collapsed flat, like a well-sprung mouse-trap, accompanied by oaths and shrieks of anger from Honners. As I instinctively ran forward to his assistance I could discern Honners' shape bulging various parts of the canvas as though he was wrestling some monster within.

He was screaming, "Get me out! Get me out! There're more nets in here than at Lord's cricket ground! Holy mackerel—that just about sums up my position!"

I was appalled to find my friend enmeshed in nets as well as in the canvas of our tent, so that the more he struggled the more he became tied up like a living parcel. Lieutenant Titterton broke cover to rush forward shouting, "Come out of there, you malicious little clown! The Japanese have obviously booby-trapped the tents. Come out at once I say! You could well trigger off a mine!"

"Then for pity's sake haul me out, nets and all!" Honners shrieked. "I'm stuck upside-down in a kind of horror-film knitting basket!"

At that moment the Japanese showed their hand. I saw the familiar grey uniforms racing over the terrain in a semi-circle amid the terrifying racket of automatic fire-power. To my left Lieutenant Titterton went down as though his legs had been shot away from under him, while behind me Honners was screaming something about not shooting a defenceless Minister of the Church who hadn't had time to find his vestments.

Then I remember going down under the fusilade of lead, being hit in the head and right shoulder almost simultaneously. The battle, such as it was, had ended.

I knew I was in Heaven because an angel was bending over the white sheet and red blanket that covered me. Then I realized the angel was Pamela. "Did they kill you as well?" I asked.

Pamela smiled at me with a mixture of relief and understanding. "So glad you've come round, Peter. You've had a tough time of it."

"Where am I then?"

"You've come back to me at last, safely on board the *Panacea*."

"Did the Japs capture the *Panacea* too, Pamela?"

"Don't tire yourself, darling. You've been quite badly knocked out. Sleep as much as you can."

I found I was bandaged round the head and over the right ear and my right shoulder was strapped up. "Did you get the bullets out already?" I inquired.

"Not bullets, dear. You were a victim of the worst hazard on these islands—you were hit by a coconut."

"A coconut! Come off it, Pamela. The Japs hosed me with tracer shells."

"No, Peter. A windfall dropped from a sixty-foot palm, knocked you out, flattened your ear badly and broke your collarbone. You know the weight of those husks—it's a miracle you weren't killed."

"I suppose the Japs thought I had been shot, so they left me for dead on the ground. It's an ill wind that blows nobody any good, eh?"

Pamela took my free hand and kissed my good ear "There weren't any Japs, Peter," she whispered.

"But we were surrounded by them!"

"They were Lieutenant Tudor's mob dressed up."

"Tudor's Section!"

Pamela nodded. "You know this feud between Tudor and Titterton better than I do. Apparently Lieutenant Tudor boasted that not only would Titterton's attack fail but also Tudor would actually capture Titterton in his own base. A kind of double victory. Well, he did just that—and Colonel Tank has recommended him for promotion to Captain."

"What's he recommended Titterton for—Corporal?"

"No, he's commended Titterton for a good scheme plus zealous leadership right to the bitter end."

"What happened to Honners?"

Pamela glanced sideways. "He's in that bed next to yours —heavily sedated for shock. You'll hear him in a minute because he seems to imagine he's some kind of Bishop. Keeps calling out for me to ring the bell for Requiem Mass. Did he ever tell you he was going to be ordained into the Church?"

"No, love," I replied, kissing Pamela gratefully, "but if he ever does we'll get him to marry us."

Pamela returned my kiss warmly until we were interrupted by a stern cry from the next bed. "Where the devil is my Padre's uniform! I refuse to conduct the service dressed in these blasted issue pyjamas!"

"Honners is getting back to normal, Peter," Pamela smiled.

"So am I, darling," I grinned, pulling her towards me so strongly that for a moment she forgot she was duty nurse.

"This could well be the turning point of the war that Winston Churchill is always on about!"

THE END

If you enjoyed reading "Marine Pook Esquire",
you can follow more of Pook's adventures in
"Pook Sahib".

An extract follows.

POOK SAHIB

O N E

"We're rolling into Shaggapore Station, Peter," Honners cries delightedly. "Just think of it—you're actually in Shaggapore at last!"

I think about Shaggapore and try to appear excited, but fail miserably. The pleasure of meeting Honners again after so long has worn thin during the endless train journey from Naval Headquarters at Jawanagar through the ancient State of Ramsam. At the moment it does not feel so much like the completion of a journey as that I am being pensioned off after a lifetime on the railways.

I little suspect that ahead of me lies one of the most mysterious epics of the war—so secret that even today I am not permitted to reveal how we came to be involved in this classic maritime adventure conducted by the landlocked State of Ramsam, and disclosed here for the very first time. Himself sworn to secrecy, Honners has hinted that yet another British officer may be connected with the assignment—none other than Commander Bray, late of the Merchant Service, whose brillant seamanship is already a legend throughout the repair yards of the East.

Link that illustrious name with Honners as Navigating Officer, and myself as crack diver of the Fleet, and you have a trio which prompted the *Ramsami Intelligence* to observe that such a formidable combination is sufficient to strike fear into the hearts of friend and foe alike.

At Shaggapore Terminus we are met by several Ramsami Rail Transport Officers who are obviously delighted to have

a train to fuss over. They warn us that the Commodore of the Navy is waiting to greet us. His title is Commodore Gooji, and we espy him afar surrounded by his aide-de-camp and retinue. Honners informs me that a Commodore is entitled to a staff of thirty subordinates whose official designations sound like brand names of detergent powders.

The chief R.T.O. performs the elaborate introduction ritual, without which it is impossible to meet anybody in Ramsam. Hence we are all saluting and salaaming as though we have nervous tics until eventually the Commodore breaks through the interminable ceremony by saying, "Ah, so you are the notorious Lieutenant Pook, the human crab, without whom the Fleet cannot sail. Salaam, Pook Sahib."

Immediately the air is again thick with salaaming hands and arms, reminding me of picnickers attacked by bees.

"So, Pook Sahib, I trust you remembered to change trains at Tippee?" the Commodore inquires by way of small talk.

"No, sir, I stayed on the train while they altered the rails," I tell him bitterly, to forestall further Ramsami badinage.

However, everybody laughs, declaring me to be a typical British Sahib of the first water who jokes in the face of adversity. Simultaneously they point to their heads, but just as I am about to take them up on this rude gesture Honners informs me that they are admiring my golden coiffure.

"We are wishing to ascertain how you tuck such luxuriant curls inside your diving-helmet, Lieutenant Pook," the Commodore says.

"I force them in with my enormous hands," I reply, holding up those fists which, as you may recall, put Fireman Tucker away in the third round after he had made a similar remark during our memorable encounter at Southampton.

Fortunately we are diverted by distant shouts of, "Down

with British Imperialism!" and "The English must go!" being chanted outside the station. Just as I begin to wonder if these are the local reaction to my arrival Commodore Gooji explains, "Ah, our impulsive students are on the march. What a grand sight to greet you as you enter Shaggapore for the first time, Lieutenant Pook."

"Quit Ramsam! Down with the British Parasite! Long live the Japanese!" echo the strident cries of the students. "Give us back our country! We demand Independence! Clear out, English Pig!"

"Come, let us watch our brave students demonstrating," the Commodore shouts excitedly, leading the way to the window in the R.T.O.'s office. "We shall be just in time to see them pouring by as they march on the British Embassy."

From the balcony it is an impressive sight to see such enthusiasm among the young as they stamp past with banners demanding the removal of the British Raj's heel from the neck of prostrate Ramsam. The students catch sight of the Commodore's flamboyant uniform and shout up at him, "Down with the British Tyrant! Up with the Japanese Liberator!"

"Hang the English Dogs!" the Commodore roars back at them.

"We want Independence!" the R.T.O. Officers chorus vigorously.

But shouting loudest of all is Honners at the rear. "Kick the British out!" he screams, throwing back his head to obtain more volume. "Away with Imperialism! Ramsam for the Ramsamis! Shoot the rotten Limeys! Hooray! . . ."

There is so much noise and shouting that nobody hears Honners hit the floor as I clout him with my business hand. Dazedly he tries to sit up as he wonders what has thumped him so effectively, but the sobering experience has completely taken his mind off his rabble-rousing activities.

"Who the hell done me?" he keeps repeating vaguely.

"I done you, mate—and you'll get done again if you start the Quit Ramsam war-chant once more. I can understand the locals getting worked up, but you and I are supposed to be English—with a war on our hands, don't forget. I haven't been here ten minutes and there's you screaming your head off for booting us out of the country. You must be off your rocker."

Honners picks himself up and groans miserably. "You've got it all wrong, Peter. The students march on the British Embassy whenever Foreign Aid is getting as low as the plughole, so everyone joins in for the hell of it. Actually they're terrified at the mere mention of Independence— they'd be bankrupt in a week—but the odd demonstration keeps the British Government on its toes and shakes up the coffers. If the students do the American Embassy next week you must come along—it's worth seeing. In fact we'll make up a party and join in. We all clench our fists and sing the *Red Flag*—that brings the dollars in as fast as sin. We never parade outside the Russian Embassy because they won't send any money—only leaflets and more diving gear."

I try to absorb the ramifications of international intrigue as best I can, so all I say is, "But the war, Honners— remember? What about the Jap Fleet steaming west across the Indian Ocean? What about the *Soonong* waiting for me so she can streak out through the Bay of Bengal like a speedboat on a mercy dash. . . ?"

"Ah, my honoured guest, now what do you think of our brave students?" rumbles the voice of Commodore Gooji who has at last torn himself away from the balcony. "What spirit, what patriotism beats within their youthful bosoms! Welcome to Shaggapore—the gayest city in all Ramsam. Tonight we are holding a Grand Mobilization Ball at the Imperial Shaggapore Gymkhana, Pook Sahib. Not often do we of the Orient have the human crab among us—therefore we make the most of you with a great feasting. All the Naval Staff will be there, so you shall meet Commander Bray and a hundred other lions of the deep. Then tomorrow we shall inspect the new diving-bell the Russians have so kindly given us for use on board the *Soonong,* and you can have a word with Commander Bray about the mighty bathysphere our Nawab is at present endeavouring to borrow from the French Government for your convenience."

"But I was under the impression it was all go, sir—boilers bursting and full steam ahead," I protest, deeming it wise at present not to delve further into the matter of diving-bells, bathysphere and conveniences.

"Ha, ha! All go!—delightful Western expression, Pook Sahib. All go it is indeed—all go to the Grand Mobilization Ball. Of course you would be at sea tonight but one cannot possibly sail during the Festival of Pijee, as you know."

The company hiss and hold up their hands at the prospect of a ship leaving port during the Festival of Pijee. Apparently such a vessel would founder like a brick.

"Then when do we sail?" I inquire hopelessly.

"Immediately after the Festival of Pijee of course, provided the ship has been blessed by the Gondahs. As sophisticated as you are, Pook Sahib, you of all people would not countenance embarking on a hazardous voyage of war in an unblessed ship during a time of religious celebration—that I will wager on."

"Preposterous notion," Honners chimes in strongly.

"Peter is not such a fool as he looks—he knows better than to flout the basic code of naval strategy."

What worries me now is that even to me it is beginning to sound like a preposterous notion I have been guilty of suggesting. In fact in my present fatigued state it appears impossible for the *Soonong* ever to sail again—always assuming that there was a time in the past when the overwhelming requirements of the Navy were satisfied to such an extent that she was permitted to leave the jetty.

"Meanwhile, Pook Sahib, you will be quartered at the Hotel Independence, because, as you are probably aware, no Europeans are permitted on board ship after sunset during the Festival of Pijee—for obvious reasons."

"No lights? What about Commander Bray then?"

"He also is staying at the Hotel Independence, together with all European officers of the Fleet. You will remain there until the Festival of Toolu commences, when naturally you will be enabled to live on the *Soonong.*"

"Who is Toolu, for pity's sake?"

"Toolu is Pijee's brother. It is during the Festival of Toolu that the Gondahs will bless your ship prior to sailing."

The whole complicated set-up is too much for me in my present state, and already my mind is subconsciously toying with the idea of asking for a posting to N.H.Q., so I cry "Enough", and let Honners put me in a horse-drawn tonga which waddles round to the Hotel Independence, my temporary quarters.

En route I notice with what pleasure is left to me that the sidewalks are liberally sprinkled with some of the most attractive girls I have ever seen. They hip along so upright that one automatically imagines them carrying pots on their heads of shimmering black hair, and they have the habit of

suddenly raising their eyes to get you in their sights like marksmen at Bisley. I smile at every one who passes and in return they laugh gaily, acknowledging my attention with that delightful Ramsami gesture of holding the nose between thumb and index finger.

Fortunately I am almost immune from their wiles, having overcome the lusts of the body by means of violent physical exercise, beautiful thoughts, and an absorbing hobby. This latter occupation is photography, but it must be admitted that recently my album seems to contain nothing except pictures of girls. Furthermore, since coming to the East I have witnessed my violent physical exercises narrow to the field of dancing, and the beautiful thoughts have had to be abandoned completely since I read Freud.

Nevertheless I take careful stock of the female situation for future investigation in the realms of photography, but when I reflect that the ritual involved in meeting one of these lovelies must be so complex and lengthy as to be next to impossible I fall asleep in the tonga.

. . . . *Continued in "Pook Sahib", which can be ordered from all good bookshops or direct from Emissary Publishing.*